For the love of Harry

Harry

Angela Bea

Other books by Angela Bea

Sam Leaves Home

(A teenage girl runs away from home to find a new life in Germany, for girls aged 13+)

Pierre's Adventures – the King's Messenger

(A mystical adventure story set in France, for boys and girls aged 11+)

Adventure in Rio

(A story written for foreign language students aged 15+, about two young people on a gap year journey in South America)

The Healthy-life-ways series

Natural pregnancy and childcare

Keeping your children healthy

Stroppy teenagers

When I am old I will wear purple

Health and Holism

Right thinking Right doing

Self-help Fibromyalgia, 'your body will heal itself'

Available on Amazon and Kindle

www.healthy-life-ways.co.uk

Dedication and disclaimer

This book is dedicated to my dear son, and to all young men who bravely and unwittingly join the Forces to become soldiers, airmen or sailors, and in so doing experience pain and disillusionment.

My apologies for any inaccuracies in the details of this book; it is not intended to offend or undermine the work of the Marines.

All the names and incidents in this book are purely fictional and linked in no way to living people.

Chapter 1

Annie turned sharply out of the gateway of the barracks with a squeal of tyres and turned left onto the road towards Exmouth. The soldier on guard at the gate watched her go with a look of slight amazement on his young face, and then he turned and shrugged his shoulders, staring blankly ahead of him again as he continued his duty.

She revved the engine impatiently as she joined the busy queue of traffic edging its way along the river road, going along beside the high fence, with its roll of barbed wire on the top, which marked the boundary of the camp, heading towards the sea and the town. She stared ahead of her, not seeing anything and driving automatically, with her thoughts in a whirl and her chest tight with anger.

This was it! She had decided to make a clean break of it and head for her old home, to her parents, back in the seaside town where she had grown up.

Her life had just snapped in two. She knew she could no longer continue this charade with Harry, this daily stress and trauma, which had dragged them both to a place of no return.

This time she was in total shock! She had come home from work at the insurance agency in Exeter as usual to the married quarters in the army barracks at Lympstone and had opened the front door quietly, so as not to disturb Harry, who might be resting. She had gone upstairs to change and opened the bedroom door gently, and there they were; Amanda, her best mate, and Harry lying side by side in the bed, wrapped in each other's arms. She had walked over to him then and slapped his face hard, so hard that her hand still stung from the slap. Amanda had screamed and Harry had dived under the bedclothes.

Without a word, and turning her back on them, she had rushed out of the room. Still in her work clothes she had picked up the car keys again and her handbag and driven out of the barracks, this time for good!

Her thoughts turned to her son who was still playing at his friend's house in town. She couldn't face seeing his cheerful grin just yet. She would first go to her Mum and Dad's and would try to explain, and beg a bed for the night for the two of them. It was still early anyway, Charlie would be ok for a bit yet.

As she made her way slowly into the town stopping at every set of red traffic lights, a better idea occurred to her. She would go down to the beach for a walk first to try and calm her frazzled nerves a bit and get a grip on herself.

So she took the inner ring road and was soon spinning along the sea front towards the sand dunes at the far end, where she parked the car. The November afternoon was grey and a cool wind was coming in off the sea. The tide was out and few people were on the beach; just a couple of dog walkers and a lot of seagulls and some oyster catchers trying to find something to eat on the seaweed washed up by the last storm.

She headed eastwards, towards the crumbling red cliffs, where she knew she could walk undisturbed, and was soon striding out along the long sandy beach beneath the cliffs, with the sea gently lapping on one side and the wind blowing hard in her face. She started to breathe again and then broke into a run. She ran on the firm sand until she could run no more and felt her breath coming in short gasps and the cold burning in her lungs. Tears were streaming down her face now and she brushed them off angrily.

'You bastard, you f...ing bastard!' she screamed at the top of her voice. The sound was carried away by the wind and the waves laughed at her with tinkling ripples.

She found a rock and sat down, her brain still numb. She took a few deep breaths and steadied herself. She felt the hard lumpy rock under her, cold and damp through her thin work trousers. Her feet dug into the damp sand until her pointed black shoes were full. The sand cooled her down, and her heart started to beat a little slower. Her brown shoulder length hair blew into her eyes but she held it back with her hand as she looked at the dull grey waves and the distant horizon. Slowly she started to think a little more clearly.

Amanda was her best friend. She shared everything with her; her secrets, her day to day struggles. She had told her all about Harry's troubles and Amanda had been so supportive. Last evening they had sat side by side on the grubby sofa together, while Harry was out playing squash and Annie had been explaining to Amanda about Harry's latest panic attack, and his visit to the psychologist at the hospital. Amanda had listened and been supportive. Surely she wasn't having an affair with Harry? Annie felt such an idiot and so let down.

Amanda's own husband Rod was out on tour in Afghanistan at the moment and not likely to be home for at least 7 weeks. They missed each other dreadfully. They hadn't been in married quarters long before he was sent out there.

Harry and Annie had had Amanda round for a couple of meals recently to help her along. Her children were only quite small, 3 ½ and 16 months and Amanda found being a full-time Mum in the barracks very hard. She often got ratty with the kids, and then sat and cried after they had gone to bed. She was finding it tough.

But this! Even with these problems, Harry couldn't have thought it was ok to go to bed with her, surely? Was he trying to comfort her? Was he just crazy?

After all they had been through in the last few years too; this seemed like a punch in the gut. Harry was still far from well, although he had now started doing some ground duties in the office, and his nerves were often ragged.

Annie sat there on the rock on the beach thinking. Time passed without her noticing. She remembered the very first time she had kissed Harry. It had been at the school disco when they were both in 5th form. He had shyly asked her for a dance and then another, until the music became smoochie and they were cuddling up close and she could smell his warm breath on her neck.

Then afterwards, when everyone had started to disperse after the disco, they had gone outside together and he had kissed her so tenderly under the starry sky and she had responded and they had laughed and gazed into each other's eyes.

After that they had started dating properly. Every Friday after school they would go into Exeter together on the small two-carriage train which crawled along by the river. Then they would get some chips and wander round the shops, which would be just about to close, or get a ticket for a film if they felt rich, or go and sit in the park near the castle and hold hands, laugh and tickle each other and drink a bottle of cider between them.

As the sun set, they might go to the Cathedral square where many of their friends could be found and might cadge a cigarette from someone and watch the changing colours on the warm stones and the birds circling around in the evening light.

They had been ecstatically happy then and never argued or disagreed.

By the time they left school at 16 they had both decided to try life in the marines. They had been to Cadets together and enjoyed the marching practice, the shooting, the outings and adventures. They thought they looked great in a uniform too, and looked up to the older boys who left to go into proper training.

By their 17th birthdays, which fell only 5 weeks apart, they had both completed their basic training in Lympstone Royal Marines and were being sent on specialist courses. Harry had opted to train for front line action, and Annie had started doing the telephonist/communications training on ground. She thought she would enjoy travelling but never fancied being in action somehow. They saw a lot of each other in their free time, if and when they managed to get it off together, but they lived in separate messes as they weren't married. They planned to get married just as soon as they had saved up enough money. They had formally asked the permission of their parents and it seemed like the only thing to do.

If they got time off together they would usually head back to Annie's parents' home, and chill out watching TV on the big sofa, holding hands.

Other friends of Annie were having fun mixing with all the boys and enjoying the odd fling after a party, but she and Harry went steady and never looked elsewhere.

Harry had finished his training by the time the Iraq war was nearly over. They watched the toppling of Sadam Hussein's statue with amazement. Would he be sent out on tour before they could arrange a wedding?

They had gone to the office and asked permission for a fortnight's leave together so they could get a honeymoon, and when it was agreed, they had started planning their Big Day.

It had turned out to be a gorgeous June day, and quite hot. Annie had worn a white dress which she had bought on-line at a very reasonable price. Her school friend had been her maid of honour and her little cousin the bridesmaid. Mum had done her flowers, pink roses with white freesias, and a posy for the bridesmaids too, and Harry had gone to Exeter and bought a suit at British Home

Stores, (which he had taken back next day and claimed it didn't fit properly, and had got his money back!)

The church wedding had been rather boring really with just a few close friends, and afterwards they had gone down to the Puffing Billy near the River Ex and had had loads of mock champagne and a salmon supper with just their parents. Harry's Mum hadn't come. Annie couldn't remember the last bit very well; she just remembered going upstairs in the pub and finding their room, the one overlooking the river, with a huge four-poster bed in it.

Next day they had moved their few possessions into the married quarters they had been issued. They were rather tatty and very uniform and their few bits and pieces hadn't made much impact on the four-square feel of the place. But it had been an exciting day, knowing they were now able to live together officially.

Their honeymoon had been a scrambled affair. They had got a cheap flight from Exeter airport on a Thompson's special deal and had flown out to Majorca for a fortnight. It had been very hot and she remembered getting very red sore shoulders after lying by the pool one day, and getting pretty drunk on the cheap red wine.

Harry had remained his normal cheerful loving self throughout and she had been very happy, her small world revolving entirely around the hugs and cuddles which he gave her. She would giggle and screw up her nose at him and gaze admiringly at his fit body as he swaggered up to the bar to get her another drink.

Once back home it was straight back into the office routine for her. She often looked at the thin gold band on her ring finger and twiddled it round and round when she was bored or a bit anxious about something. All the girls had admired it and wished her well.

Annie looked down at her hands now, cold in the November wind and realised she had been twiddling the ring round and round as she sat there on the rock. She had no idea how long she had sat there.

The evening sky was darkening with just a few orange streaks appearing down near the horizon, showing that the sun was setting. The tide was beginning to turn and if she stayed much longer she would be cut off at the corner where the cliffs came down close and she would have to scramble back over the rocks to save her feet getting wet.

She glanced at her watch. It was 4.15 and time for her to fetch Charlie from his friend in town. She didn't know the family very well yet, this was only the second time he had gone there to play, so she had to look normal and in control. By the time she got back to her parked car it was getting dusky and all the seagulls were flying eastwards towards their nesting places on the cliffs.

She looked at her face in the car mirror, it was pale and her nose was a little red, but otherwise passable. Then she took out her hairbrush to tidy her glossy brown hair. She put just a touch more lipstick on and checked her mascara, before starting the engine and gently backing the car onto the road, needing her headlights on now, as she drove back along the bay.

Chapter 2

When Charlie heard her at the front door of his friend's house, he ran down the hallway and gave her his normal hug and then turned and waved goodbye to Tom. He chattered happily as he scrambled into the back seat and clicked his seatbelt on.

'Surprise for you!' said Annie, 'We'll be having tea at Gran's tonight. Dad isn't too well, so we'll leave him in peace, eh?'

This was a common scenario for Charlie. Having grown up with a Dad who first was away a lot and then was constantly 'unwell' he knew that Mum was the one to whom he looked for his security, comfort and companionship. But tonight he sensed that something was not quite as usual. His 7 year old instincts were alert and he looked at his Mum in the driving mirror, trying to make out her expression in the light of the passing street lamps.

She glanced at him from time to time too. He was growing up fast and his elf-like freckled face, framed by thick ginger hair, looked vulnerable and anxious, she thought. He was doing alright at school though and his teacher was supportive and positive. It wasn't easy being a barracks kid.

They turned into the familiar road with the rows of identical 1950's semi-detached houses, where his grandparents lived, and drew up outside the house with the red front door and the fuchsia bushes still in bloom in the front garden. The No. 92 sign was not visible in the dark, but Charlie ran up the path and pushed open the front door without ringing the 'Avon calling' chime bell.

'Hi, Gran' he shouted, dropping his schoolbag on the stool in the hallway. His Grandmother appeared from the sitting room. She had been watching her favourite programme about antiques and was not too happy to be disturbed so suddenly.

She looked beyond the child to her daughter standing in the hallway, and saw her white face and pinched expression. She went over and gave her a hug and whispered,

'What's up now?'

Annie just shook her head and fought back her tears, which were threatening to well up again. She indicated to Charlie and put a finger to her lips.

'Can we stay here tonight?' she croaked, and her Mother nodded slowly, concern in her eyes.

'You go on out the back and see if Grampi needs a hand with the chickens,' she instructed her young grandson. Charlie obeyed and was soon engrossed in the gloomy back garden with his grandfather, locking the hens in for the night.

'So what's up?' said Stella softly to her daughter, once he had gone.

'I'm done with it,' said Annie, 'I found him in bed with Amanda this afternoon.'

Now it was Stella's turn to go white and she clung to her daughter as though they were both on a sinking ship.

Suddenly she pulled herself together and the practical trained nurse that 'could cope in any emergency' kicked in.

'Well, I'll get Ted to clean out his rubbish from the box room and Charlie can have that as his, while you can have the spare room with the twin beds. I'll just go up and put the clean stuff on them.'

No sooner said, than she went upstairs and started banging about in the linen cupboard on the landing, and making up the beds for her family.

Annie smiled to herself. Good old Mum could be relied on in any emergency, but she felt heaviness at being in her parent's house with no stuff of her own, completely beholden to them for everything. She wandered out to the kitchen which was just as it had always been in her memory. The gas cooker was decidedly past its sell by date and had spills from many meals on it. The ledges were all cluttered and rather grimy, the saucepans from lunch were still soaking in the sink and the cats bowl smelt bad.

She automatically reached for the kettle and filled it with water from the greasy sink. It started to hum almost immediately and she took down 3 chipped mugs from the cupboard above the cooker and Charlie's little one that he liked to use here, and put tea bags in them. The fridge on the other side of the room was also dirty and not well stocked and the milk was 3 days past its 'best before' date. She sniffed it suspiciously but it still smelt ok for a much needed cup of tea, so she added some to the steaming hot cups and stirred in a sweetener for her Mum, 2 spoons of sugar for Dad and took a healthy slurp of hers, as she badly needed it. Of course it burnt her tongue, but she took another sip, this time more carefully for good measure.

Just then Ted and Charlie appeared, laughing together and with steaming breath and pink cheeks.

'Well this is a nice surprise! It's going to be frosty tonight, so we've covered the hens with a sack for the first time this year. Brr, winter's on its way!'

He gave Annie a quick peck on the cheek and picked up his mug of tea with grimy hands.

'What brings you here tonight?' he enquired and Charlie watched his mother's face, looking for clues as the adults spoke. He wondered too.

'Oh, Harry wants a break from our chatter,' she lied. There would be plenty of time to explain, once Charlie had gone up to bed.

Just then Stella reappeared.

'Oh Ted, I need you for a moment upstairs. You know those boxes you have been meaning to put up in the attic; well they are really getting on my nerves, could we do it now d'you think? '

Ted knew better than to argue, especially in front of the child, so he followed her up the stairs with its threadbare carpet to the small box room. There Stella pushed the door shut and spoke rapidly, telling him that Annie and Charlie were here to stay and he would need to clear this lot pronto, no questions asked! He looked rather bemused but set to, taking down the loft ladder and disappearing all the stuff which had been piled up on the little single bed. As he worked steadily he began to understand this emergency and that his daughter had finally walked out on her very difficult marriage.

Their family was going to be somewhat enlarged for a while anyway. He sighed and thought about the few times when he had had arguments with Stella about trivia. Marriage wasn't always a bed of roses, but his precious only daughter had apparently pulled the short straw.

'Bloody wars' he thought! Things would be ok without them. It was all the stupid politicians fault. They shouldn't have been out in Afghanistan in the first place!

Feeling angry he went into the bathroom to wash, before descending to his beloved grandson with a big fresh smile on his face.

Chapter 3

When Amanda finally stopped screaming, Harry poked his head out from the bedclothes.

'Just get out!' he barked in his military voice.

She did not need to be told twice, but threw on her jumper and slacks and rushed out of the door, slamming it behind her, leaving Harry lying crumpled up under the thin duvet. He had nothing but his pants on and started to shiver violently. His eyes half closed he stumbled to the wardrobe and pulled on his track suit before sinking back again on the bed. His short stubbly hair, sandy coloured like his son's, was just visible on the pillow above the duvet.

He groaned as though in pain and his legs thrashed about. What had possessed him to invite Amanda round in the middle of the day? How on earth had they got to this point at all, from a cosy friendly chat on the sofa downstairs to lying side by side almost naked in the marital bed? He had needed to hold onto something or someone, as the black tunnel feeling was starting again. Once it took hold of him he was whisked backwards and out of his body like an electric train, and there was no knowing when he would return to normality again. He had come to recognise the warning signs. His stomach went tight, his hands became cold and clammy and there was a whirring noise in his head, sometimes with machine gun fire spattering as well.

It had started this morning when he had been at work in the office. He had had to take a call from one of his old squadron, whom he hadn't seen for several months. It was the Sergeant. They had exchanged a couple of pleasantries and then Rob had asked him how he was doing. Rather than brushing it off and saying, 'Fine, thanks,' he had started to tell him a bit about how the post-traumatic stress disorder was still affecting him. Once he started talking about it, it seemed as though it gave itself permission to reappear, like a stealthy cat creeping up in the night. Rob had listened politely and the chap in the office had looked across at him strangely as though to say, 'What are you wasting phone time for, chatting like that?' so he had called off abruptly. Instead of continuing his filing job in hand, he had disappeared out to the toilet and sat there for ages with the whirring noise starting in his head again.

He just had sat there, time going by, until one of his work colleagues knocked on the door and said,

'You ok in there, mate?'

No he wasn't ok! The noises were crashing in his head again and the tight feeling in his stomach was making him feel decidedly sick. He couldn't open his eyes without seeing the blood everywhere, and hearing the screaming of his best friend Eric, moments before he died. His eyes kept looking into his with that accusing look and terror worse than could be imagined.

They had been through this countless times before; Eric and he, wherever he was now? But he was certainly not at peace. Every time Harry got into this state, Eric was right there with him. He had tried talking to him, begging him to let go and leave him in peace, but it never worked.

Now the officer in charge was unlocking the toilet door from the outside and firmly lifting him off the toilet seat where he had sat for he knew not how long, with his trousers around his knees. These knees now shook as he tried to stand up. Someone else was telling him to pull himself together, someone who should be shot!

'Home time for you, Harry,' said his officer kindly, and he took a piece of paper from his desk. It was a familiar form to let him off work, and Harry managed to sign it with shaking hands.

This had happened many times in the last months. He couldn't tell when he would have to ditch out of work for a couple of days. Usually Annie was at home and would be phoned up to come across and get him. She only worked very part time now since she had given up the army work. It was more for her sanity really, to get her out into real life that she did it; just three mornings a week at the insurance company in Exeter, mainly answering phone enquiries.

But today she was still at work and wouldn't be back till after 3. His rock was not there to cling on to! The young clerk in the office, Sally, was told where he lived and what to do, so she led him in a daze back across the compound and along the road which led to the married quarters. He stumbled and shook and his head hung down, he couldn't really remember much about getting home as the hissing was still so loud in his head.

Sally was inexperienced, and just led him into their sitting room where he slumped down on the sofa. She simply left him sitting there and went back to the office.

So Harry picked up the phone and pressed the first button on the automatic key pad. He thought it would go straight through to Annie's workplace, but instead he heard Amanda's light voice at the other end. He breathed heavily and Amanda said,

'Harry is that you? Are you ok? Where's Annie? D'you want me to come over?'

He hadn't answered any of these questions coherently and Amanda realised that he needed someone urgently to be with him. So she had turned off the cooker and hurried over the road to their house, where she found the front door unlocked. Her kids were at the nursery for the morning so she wouldn't need to pick them up for another half hour at least.

She had walked straight in and Harry had managed to smile and indicate her to sit down on the sofa.

'The bloody monster is at me again, 'Manda,' he grimaced, and put his arm around her for comfort. 'When is this ever going to stop? Feel like I'm going crazy all the time!'

21

'You *will* get better, Harry. Just hang on in there, it's early days yet.'

'It feels like it's been my whole life,' Harry said ruefully, 'I can't remember life when it was normal. I do so want to get the hell out of here. Come upstairs with me, so I can lie down, will you?'

So they had gone up to the bedroom together and Harry had taken off his uniform trousers and shirt, and she had taken off her slacks and jumper, and they had got into bed together. That was it! Nothing more had happened, except he had clung onto Amanda as the whirring started again. Later, much later, they had heard steps up the stairs and Annie had walked in and found them together.

Harry groaned out loud. His face still stung where Annie had hit him. No-one could hear him; the neighbours were all at work. Now he had completely blown it, his marriage was in tatters. How could he explain all that had gone on to Annie, and convince her that finding her best friend in bed with him was not just a sexual fling, to keep him happy while she was out at work?

She had been so wonderful since he'd got back from Afghanistan. Every day she had talked to him, held his hands, brought him back from the brink of insanity, talked to the medics, talked to the office where he was now working, made excuses for him, kept him in some sort of work and had encouraged him to continue; basically she had had faith that he would get better, and now he had smashed it all!

They had been pretty decent at the work assessment; they had given him this flexible part-time job in the office with 'no stress', and allowed him to stay on in the Marines. How often did that happen? Most people got pensioned out and had to try and start a new life from scratch, with no support or accommodation. Maybe it was because they really valued them as a family? Annie had been a good worker too, and only left her job here after he got back, so she could spend more time at home. Her recent new job in Exeter was a sign that he must be improving; or maybe it was because the strain was becoming too much? Perhaps she wanted out?

He felt remorse that the girl, whom he loved so much, whom he had thought of every minute of every day while he was away, should have to suffer on his behalf. He never wanted to hurt her. This whole business was shit!

He groaned again, this time louder. Perhaps he should just go downstairs and end it all with some Paracetamol, or the gas oven? But his body wouldn't even move. He felt frozen in time and the hissing in his head wouldn't stop and was driving him to distraction!

He tried to go to sleep. He had been given tablets to help that, so maybe he could take a couple now? He rummaged in the bedside drawer till he found the foil pack and swigged down a couple of the bitter tasting tablets with some water which still stood on the bedside cabinet from last night. He curled himself into a miserable ball and waited for them to kick in. Maybe a good sleep would help him to focus again on the current dilemma. He was sure Annie would have gone home to her parents. He would try and ring her later, when he had slept this off.

Chapter 4

Harry slept deeply with the drugs inside him. He woke up in the pitch dark. He looked at his watch; it must be the middle of the night. It showed 4 a.m. He had slept for nearly 12 hours! He had a thumping headache and felt cold and thirsty, but the wretched hissing had stopped, thank goodness. He felt strangely numb and lay on his back gazing at the dark ceiling. He would go down and make a hot drink and have a sandwich, as he had missed supper.

He stumbled out of bed, feeling a bit dizzy, and nearly fell over his uniform which was lying by the bed. He put the light on and blinked in the brightness. His face, as he looked in the mirror that Annie used to apply her makeup each morning, showed up pale, with huge dark rings under his eyes. His sandy hair, cut short as ever, was thinning on top, and he had stubble of growth on his jaw. He gazed back at his reflection and mused at the changes that had happened in the last three years. He looked older than 27. He was a father of a 7 year old and had been a soldier for 9 years nearly; too long! And he was only 27 still. He felt about 60!

Going to the bathroom he looked at his tattooed arms and read the one above the elbow, a little cupid with the words 'I love you for ever, Annie'. Yes, he did still love her, and was going to get her back, if it killed him in the process.

Downstairs, knife in hand as he made a thick ham and pickle sandwich, and the kettle nearly boiling for his tea, he heard the familiar click of the cat-flap as the tabby and white moggy which had adopted them some years ago, came leaping in with a loud 'Prr' greeting! He bent down and picked her up and she started purring loudly. He nuzzled his face deep into her fur and stroked her.

'Oh, puss! You're the only friend I have now,' and a tear of self-pity trickled down his face.

With his tea and sandwich balanced on a small tray and the cat under his other arm, he mounted the stairs again and got back into bed. The cat immediately started kneading the bedclothes, purring ecstatically. Harry munched on his sandwich and put on the small radio beside the bed with his favourite music. He normally liked heavy metal, an angry sound, but today it jarred, so he switched over to Classic FM, which he had only recently discovered and he listened enchanted to Bach's "Air on a G string" which he had never heard before. He took a deep breath and a big swig of his strong tea.

A thought occurred to him. He rummaged again in the bedside drawer and eventually found a leather bound notebook that Annie had given him last Christmas. She hadn't said anything to him then, but he had put it away realising that one day he would want to write in it. She had given him a really nice pen too, which was easy on the hand and flowed well. He kept that with the book for the right moment. Now was the right moment! He wasn't usually alone at night, Annie would be gently breathing beside him if he did wake up in the dark, and he would put his arms around her for comfort. Now he only had the cat, which had made itself comfortable down near his feet, and had gone to sleep curled up.

He opened the notebook on this first white page and looked at it. His mind was slightly foggy from the tablets, but all signs of the previous days panic had gone now. He was just left with a huge pain in his chest, such sadness he could hardly bear it. He rubbed his chest gently to relieve the pain and picked up his pen.

Thursday 10th November. (He wrote at the top)

'I was always sure I wanted to be a soldier, even when I was a kid! My friends and I used to play at being soldiers where we lived down near the sea front at Exmouth. We would play along the sand-dunes and would ambush each other, and shoot with toy rifles made out of drift-wood. Eric was my best mate. I had always known him. He lived down the road from me, and his Mum and mine had been at the hospital together to give birth to us. So he was like a brother really!'

He paused briefly chewing the pen and reread what he had written. He wasn't used to this writing business, but he would keep trying.

'Eric has a sister too, but I was an only child. I often went to his house to play and we would watch TV and fiddle about in his room with his Lego, and his books on aeroplanes and his toys. He had some small plastic soldiers too and we would line them up for battle and move them round and kill some of them off too. It was good fun killing them and we would have mock battles and blood, which we made from tomato ketchup nicked from his Mum.

'Sometimes at a weekend there would be a parade in town, usually for the Remembrance service and we would watch the soldiers marching by to lay their wreaths. Or we would hear the shooting at Sandy Bay, where they have a rifle range and the soldiers all practice. Or we would see the chinook helicopters flying over the estuary, practicing low level flights. Sometimes when we took a bus to Exeter with our Mums we would pass the barracks at Lympstone and ask our Mums what happened in there and what the soldiers were doing.

'By the time we were twelve we had made a blood brother pact to become soldiers. We had made a tiny cut on our fingers and rubbed our blood together, making this a magic moment. We had worked out a secret code too and we sat down and wrote a message, then rubbed it with special wax so it disappeared. We had got the kit in the trick shop down in town.

'We hid that piece of paper in a jar in the bottom of the hollow tree in Eric's garden, knowing that only we would ever find it again.

'When I started dating Annie, Eric had been a bit jealous at first and we had drifted apart a bit, but by the time we were on our last bit of cadet training course, he had got used to the idea that we were a threesome and we had had some great times together at camp. We had all enrolled at Lympstone at the same time, and joy of joys, we ended up in the same squadron, so we could have drinks in the bar together, chats in our mess in our time off and go on training exercises over the Commons together. Eric was a good

Marine and strong too. He often put himself forward to go that extra mile, and he was the Sergeant's favourite.

'After we had done all the various parts of our training, we heard that a lot of troops were being sent out to Afghanistan. I had hardly heard of the place and looked it up on the internet. It said there had been a war going on there for ages with the Russians, who had now gone, but that now a group called the Taliban were fighting there. The people were suffering, so England, with its idealistic view that it could protect the whole world, was sending out troops to Kabul to 'stabilize' the area. There would be no fighting, no shooting, they told us!

'I realised too that the Taliban had apparently sent the planes which crashed into the twin towers on 9/11, so they were also America's enemy. (Although, since then, I have watched an uTube documentary, which suggested the whole thing was a set-up job! I don't know what to believe really, except that war is always there and there have to be jobs for us boys! We must all be idiots!)'

Harry paused in his writing for a moment, chewing his pen again, and smiled ruefully at himself. All this suffering was of his own making! He had chosen to become a soldier and had always wanted to fight. It was exhilarating and scary at the same time. It made one feel invincible. He remembered the many times he had seen the stretchers being rushed over to the C17's on the dusty runway at Camp Bastion to be transported back to the big hospitals in Europe. Blown off limbs, blindness, and worse than that; a corpse.

That was before they had an f...ing hospital in Camp Bastion, which could do any patch-up job from those lethal IEDs (Improvised Explosive Devises). He steered his brain away from the gruesome images which flashed like a slide show across his tired inner eyes. He couldn't dwell there, although he had seen much. Where had he got to? He reread what he had written in his slightly shaky hand, draining his mug of what was now cold tea.

He glanced at the alarm clock. It was already 7.15 a.m. and there was a dull glow outside, indicating another cold grey day. He didn't need to get up; he was signed off for two days at least so could carry on writing. Where had he got to?

'Eric and I stood in front of the OC in the Lympstone rain with the others in our squadron. He barked out that we would be going to Afghanistan, that we would be out there about six months, and we would be issued with our kit in a few days. He said a lot more which I can't remember. I was just thinking of Annie. I would have to tell her gently tonight that I was going away. It was inevitable really and she had been expecting it, but now it was for real. No more nightly cuddles, no laughing in the morning as we put on our uniforms.

'Annie had felt a bit queasy the last few mornings. She also had missed her last period. She had just made an appointment with the Doctor to check if she was actually pregnant. We had been thrilled, if she was really carrying our first child! And that same day I was called up! What were the Heavens thinking? That was really unfair. I wanted to be close so I could experience the wonder of her swelling belly and see the tiny foetus fluttering inside her when she went for her scans. I wanted to be a proactive Dad, and now I had to go away just as it was starting. I should be back for the birth, but that was a lifetime away.

'Annie seemed to take it well, but I could hear her silently crying after we had kissed goodnight and put the light out. I couldn't

29

bear to let her know I heard her, because she had to be brave. I wasn't; I felt cold fear in my gut, and was dreading picking up that kit and flying out of Brize Norton next Tuesday to the temporary camp they had set up in the desert.

'They told us it would be hot in the day and cold at night; thermals then? Our equipment was basic; we had no proper vests then, not until they had had a few go down with a bullet in their chests. 32 had been killed that first year! There was uproar over that, but a lot of our stuff was inadequate for the job in hand. Economy cutting doesn't work when you have a desperate local Taliban out to get you!

'On the day we left, Annie had to go into work as usual, so she couldn't come to Brize to see us off like some of the other wives and mothers did. It was all so emotional! After a while people got more used to it, and said their goodbyes in private at home, but this first time it was different. The BBC were filming too, how crass! Couldn't they give us the privacy we deserve?

'She had given me a small packet to unwrap when I got out there. It got through the security scanner ok, so it must be something fairly innocuous. I opened it when finally I was in my small cramped tent that night. It was stuffy and humid in there, but outside the temperature was dropping rapidly. When I poked my head out I saw the most amazing clear sky full of stars so bright you could almost touch them!

'In the rather dim light of my issue torch I found a few photos, those of us having fun on holidays, holding hands, laughing. She had also put in an LED wind-up torch and a large slab of my favourite dark nut chocolate. What a great girl! Inside a little box there was also a small locket on a chain with a tiny bit of her shiny brown hair inside. That would bring me good luck! She had had it engraved with, 'Annie loves you lots!' I kissed it tenderly, as I would many times in the next months. It was the only bit of her I had now. Inside her our small son would be growing too. We were now a family! I had to hang on to that, whatever shit I met out here.'

Harry's mind started wandering, and he stopped writing. He felt the small cat moving on his feet and it brought him back to reality. He felt desperately tired again, so he put down the notebook and pen on the bedside locker, and snuggled under the duvet. It didn't matter if he slept a bit again. He wasn't hungry and he felt slightly more relaxed now. So he put his head down and drifted off into a light daytime sleep, while the cat purred like a steam train down by his feet.

Chapter 5

Charlie woke up in the little bed in his Gran's house and looked around him. He felt great after a good night's rest and wanted to get up, but he hadn't got any clean clothes and Mum hadn't said anything about getting them. It must be nearly time to get up anyway, so he slipped out of bed and put on his yesterday's school clothes which were on the chair.

He hadn't got anything to play with or read either, so he tiptoed quietly over to the bathroom and then crept downstairs to get himself a bowl of cereal from the kitchen cupboard. He was hungry so he put plenty of Rice Crispies in the bowl, tipping some onto the table by mistake.

He would go out in the garden before Grampi got up and surprise him by feeding the hens. Perhaps he might find an egg or two as well?

He was just tucking into his breakfast when he heard his Mum coming quietly down the stairs.

'You're up with the larks,' she teased. 'Have you found something nice to eat?'

He nodded, and then forgetting his manners he said with a full mouth,

'When we go home later, I'll have to get my homework book for Miss Aitkin. I left it in my room by mistake yesterday.'

Annie sat down beside him, and looked at his freckled face and blue/green eyes that looked so like Harry's.

'We won't be going back to the camp for a while, love. Dad's not well, so we've got to stay here for a bit and make do as best we can. I can't go back to get your stuff either, so I'll go shopping today for a few bits and pieces. You can manage ok can't you, like being on holiday? Try to help Mum as much as you can. It's not going to be easy.'

She kissed the top of his head as she got up to put the kettle on. Soon her parents would be down and the quiet intimacy she enjoyed with Charlie would be gone, as they fussed around him, before he headed out for the day. He was an amiable lad and enjoyed visiting his grandparents generally, but what would he be like, when he realised that he was not going back home again?

His relationship with his father was a unique one. Because he had only seen him intermittently as he grew up, there were huge expectations of his absent Dad; someone to play with, someone to show his new things to, someone to be a 'mate'; not really a strict father figure, or a parental role model. He loved him dearly though and when Charlie saw his Dad on the sofa with an agonised expression on his face and his fists clenched, and a distant look in his eyes he would quietly go over and instinctively put a small hand on his knee or sit up close beside him, resting his head on his shoulder, rather like a devoted dog might its master.

He was very like Harry in many ways, but he had also got his mother's strength of character and sense of humour. He was a thoughtful boy and an easy mixer, despite being an only child. Quite often he would say to his Mum,

'Can't I have a little sister to play with?' It was always a sister he wanted, not a brother!

Mum would laugh lightly and say,

'When Dad is better maybe.'

Now Charlie got up and put his bowl in the dishwasher. He put on his wellies which he kept by the back door and slipped out into the cold morning mist, with only his blue school jumper on. The hens crooned gently as he took the sack off their nesting box. They were still in bed, two of them, so he houshed them out of the nesting box as his Grampi had shown him, and there underneath were three lovely warm eggs. He would ask if he could eat one now!

Clutching them carefully, he walked back to the kitchen and opened the door into the bright warm space. Gran was down there too now and preparing the sandwiches for his lunchbox. He liked her lunches; she always put in a treat, like a chocolate bar, or a bag of crisps. His Mum didn't let him have these, as it wasn't healthy.

'What have you found? Have the hens been laying you some breakfast?' she smiled over at him and indicated he should sit down at the table. Her no-nonsense approach made him feel secure and at ease. He knew what would be expected of him at each moment. Sometimes his Mum got annoyed that Gran was so strict, but it didn't bother him. He liked her blunt ways.

Once the fresh egg was boiled and Gran had made him some bread and butter soldiers with Marmite to go with it, he tucked in silently while his Mum and Gran planned their day out together in Exeter. (Mum not working today? It was Thursday and she usually worked.) They would drop him off at the school on the way, as Mum wanted to see the headmistress (Why, he hadn't done anything naughty?), then stop at the Barracks to see the OC (not get his school book?) and then go by her workplace, (without stopping to work there?)

It was all rather confusing, so he concentrated on his delicious egg and had a joke with Grampi when he appeared, smelling of shaving cream with little wisps of white foam still hanging round the edges of his face. Grampi was mischievous like him and would do funny or silly things when Gran had her back turned. Now he just winked at him and waggled his ears. Charlie wished he could do both these things, but as much as he practised in front of the mirror he couldn't make it work!

Grampi would stay home today. It would be a nice peaceful day for him to read the paper, look at the snooker and potter in the garden when it warmed up a bit. The sky was clear so it might be sunny later on. He enjoyed a day alone at home. Stella was awfully chatty sometimes!

'Can you sort the dishes, Ted,' she now bossed him. 'I'm going with Annie to the school and then on to Exeter to see her boss. We'll do some shopping while we're there.'

She gave Ted a meaningful look, and he sighed, while Annie whispered to Charlie that he should brush his teeth now as it was nearly time to go.

Once in the car they made their way through the morning rush hour traffic towards his school. He liked school and found learning easy. He was annoyed though that his homework was back at Dad's and he might have a detention or something if he didn't give it in.

Miss Aitkin was quite a strict teacher but really cool, and the thought of upsetting her was far worse than the dawning reality that now he was living with his grandparents. He just looked out of the window and sneakily sucked his thumb, hoping that Gran wouldn't turn round and spot him. They thought he had grown out of doing it.

Mum took him to the classroom block, while Gran waited in the bulging car park, and then once she had seen him into his classroom, Annie slipped quickly down the corridor towards the headmistress's office.

It always reminded her of her childhood, going to stand in front of the big desk and admitting to some wrong-doing. Today she had real butterflies in her stomach, but it was important that the school knew what was happening to Charlie, in case he was disruptive or disturbed in any way. There was always good communication between the staff and parents here.

'Good morning,' she started hesitatingly, as the weary headmistress had her head down looking at some books on her desk.

She looked up at Annie and smiled; a nice young woman and going through a difficult patch, too. She hoped there was no bad news about her husband?

Annie spoke fast and rather incoherently. She didn't give all the details of her shock yesterday. They didn't have to know the gruesome details; enough just to say that she was leaving Harry and would be staying for a short while with her parents.

'Oh, I'm so sorry to hear that,' sympathized the head mistress. 'We'll keep an eye out for Charlie in case he gets upset. I expect he'll miss his Dad.'

Annie nodded silently then backed out of the room with a hurried, 'Well, goodbye now'.

She briefly touched her Mum's hand for comfort once she was back at the steering wheel. Stella understood how difficult everything was and for once in her life wasn't giving a running commentary on it!

They headed along the river road towards the Barracks and showed their passes as they came to a halt at the entrance gate. Annie felt like an automaton going through an exercise. Her army training helped her at these moments.

Without looking over to the left where the married quarters were she drove straight over to the office block and parked outside the large grey building, in a visitors space.

'Do you want me to come in too?' asked Stella.

'I think I'll manage it,' croaked Annie with a dry throat, 'but thanks all the same.'

She made her way up the cold concrete staircase till she came to the office marked **OC Templeton,** half way along the long corridor and paused briefly before giving a rapid knock.

'Come in', said a sharp military voice after a brief pause. As she entered she recognised the OC at the large desk. He was not an unpleasant man and knew her already from her many visits to sign Harry in and out of work. He had been very supportive and kept Harry on when at times he was not fit to continue.

'Oh, good morning Mrs Kenny!' he now said with a smile, 'How can I help you today? Is Harry feeling any better? He was rough yesterday morning when I sent him off. The youngster who was new here took him home and said she just left him sitting on the sofa. I was a bit concerned that you weren't home yet.'

Annie gulped before replying. So he knew that Harry was rough? What had happened exactly yesterday to get Amanda in bed with him? Was she missing some vital clue?

'I just came to tell you that I'm leaving him,' she said hurriedly, 'Yesterday it was the last straw, and I've moved out temporarily to my parents in Exmouth with Charlie. Here is my phone and address there should you wish to contact me urgently. My post could be forwarded there too.'

'Oh, Mrs Kenny, I'm truly sorry to hear that. Would you like an appointment to speak with the padre at all? I am sure Harry will miss you dreadfully. We'll do all we can to support him still.'

With this show of human concern Annie just stood there dumbly, tears pricking the back of her eyes. She couldn't break down in here. She would have to get back down to her Mum in the car before she lost the plot!

'Thank you for your help. Goodbye,' was all she could muster, and backed out of the office and almost ran down the corridor and down the musty stairs.

The fresh cold air hit her and she took great gulps of it as she walked towards the car where her Mum was reading a magazine she had found in the door pocket. She now looked up expectantly and smiled at Annie. She could see from her white face that it hadn't been easy.

As Annie got in she handed her a fresh white tissue from the little packet she always carried in her handbag. Annie gripped the steering wheel with both hands until the knuckles went white and leant her head down on it. Her shoulders shook and she silently sobbed as she had never sobbed before.

After a few minutes with her Mum gently stroking her head, Stella suggested,

'Take a few deep breaths, dear and have a good belly laugh! It always helps!'

Annie looked at her strangely, but lifted her head and smiled, then started laughing. At first it was a bit forced and she was still crying at the same time, but eventually the great tension in her stomach started to ease as she and Stella laughed together with great belly laughs. They couldn't stop and the little car was rocking on its wheels in the carpark.

A soldier walked passed quickly and looked at them strangely, which brought them both to their senses.

Both Stella and Annie wiped their tears, and Annie started the engine again.

'Next stop, the Insurance Company,' she said as she drove up though the front gate of the Barracks. She got safely out onto the road, taking more care than she had yesterday and drove towards Exeter without a backwards glance at the married quarters sitting there in the morning light. She sensed Harry was at home, but he hadn't seen her come and go. He was sleeping peacefully.

Chapter 6

Harry woke up with a start. His heart was pounding and he had hissing in his ears, but he wasn't going down that tunnel again! The clock said 9.45 and the sun was streaming into the room. He had only slept for a couple of hours. It was just an escape really. He wasn't tired any more.

So he picked up the pen again and opened the notebook. He read the bit he had written earlier, and then launched himself once more onto the page.

'We weren't in those tents very long. Once Camp Bastion had started to get established we were transferred over there. We liked having a proper roof over our heads and there were cool things on camp, like the bar, the gym, and the burger shop. It was huge there. It took 35 minutes in the trucks to cross the compound, like a big town really. There were soldiers from many countries there but we stuck together with our squadron pretty much and trained hard.

'The camp was blisteringly hot and dry and our eyes got really sore from the wind and sand when it came up. We would wrap cloth around our noses and mouths and stay inside if possible. The sky got really grey on those days, but at other times the sun shone down relentlessly.

'Every day we would have to go on a 'reccy' out into the countryside beyond the camp. The Taliban were all around us and we needed to root them out. We would generally walk in single file with our guns at the ready and our vests and helmets on. Our sergeant was Rob. He was a good bloke and realised that we were scared. At 19, when you have never been on tour before, it can be scary! We didn't know what to expect from the Taliban insurgence. We didn't recognise them from the many peasants we saw wandering along the dusty tracks and across the fields of crops. They all seemed to look the same, drab long clothes, cloth wrapped around their heads and a beard.

'We often had to jump across the irrigation ditches between the fields of grain and got wet and muddy (rather like the French trenches). The villages were surrounded by high mud walls and we had to walk between them along narrow alleyways with no visibility. What was on the other side of that wall? The chinook helicopters were our backup. We could radio them if we needed some help, or a man went down.

'The first time we were involved in fire with the enemy we were on the edge of a big field. We saw them in the distance and spotted their weapons. We let rip with our ammunitions, just firing like crazy in their direction. It was exhilarating; just like we used to play in the sand-dunes as kids! I loved the hot noisy gun in my arms, vibrating and spattering and it gave me such a sense of power.

'We had practised before for many hours of course, getting our aim as good as possible, but this was for real at last! There was an enemy and we were going to get them! The adrenalin was pumping! Afterwards when we were back in camp we bragged about the one we had shot down. It didn't occur to me until much later that I had just killed a man.

'Our toilets on camp were pretty basic at first. We had oil drums with a seat attached; they stank! If you did anything wrong you got put on 'poo duty,' that meant going out and burning it! I had to do it a couple of times. I can still remember the acrid smell of that poo burning! It was a shit job!

'Our squad had 30 soldiers, most of them great guys, all about 19 when we started. We all had a laugh and shared our fags and chocolate if someone got a parcel from home. Annie was great and wrote nearly every week. She told me about the little things, what Charlie was doing, when he started sleeping through, when his first tooth came through, when he started crawling.

'I had got leave to come home around the time of his birth and so I always thought of him as that squidgy little bundle that he was as a new-born. It is amazing becoming a father. You don't realise until it happens. That little thing has been created by my sperm! He used to look up at me with such trust in his eyes; then he learnt to smile. I had to leave him with Annie. The two most precious things in my life were thousands of miles away, while I was in this heat and dust; they were in the barracks, in an institution having to toe the line and wait and wait and wait for my safe return. How selfish of me not to realise what it was doing to them! I was missing out on the most precious times with my son, my firstborn.

'Often after a hard day, once I had cleaned up and got my smelly hot uniform off, I would strip down and lie on the top of my bed, and gaze at Annie's picture and hold the locket in my hand and kiss it and masturbate. I missed her so much! I would look carefully at the pictures of Charlie which she sent with her letters, and think about them both at home.

'Occasionally I got to speak to them. There was a queuing system for the crackling phone on camp. You were only allocated a small number of calls, and never if there had been an incident. Then everything shut down and you were on high alert. Annie would sound relieved to hear my voice when I did get through, but our conversations were a bit stilted, like you didn't have much to say to each other.

'My mate Eric was doing better emotionally than I was. He didn't have a kid, although he had been dating a girl seriously before he was sent out. He used to tease her on the phone and make sexy comments to the lads about his 'bit of stuff' back home. Eric was good with me though. Sitting on my bed in the small room which was our only privacy we would chat about Exmouth. He missed his Mum more than I did. My mum was a funny lady who had her own mind about things. Yes, I loved her, but I didn't feel that close.

'My parents had split up when I was 11 and I had gone to live with my Dad who was often at work, so I became very emotionally independent as a teenager. At least I thought I was very grown up, dating Annie and all. But I realise now she was my surrogate Mum too!

'I had often gone round to Eric's place if I wanted a bit of ordinary family life. His younger sister was fun to be with too. His Mum and I got on famously. She wrote to Eric nearly every time there was a post delivery and used to send him homemade cake sometimes, a really rich fruit cake which was a bit gooey in the middle.

'We sat on my bed together and ate cake and moaned about various staff who we thought were nerds!'

Harry stopped writing and Eric came close. He breathed deeply and shied away from the accusing eyes, the smell of blood, and the voice which was always the same, just as he remembered him. This time he was not going to panic and flip out in fear. Eric was real, he was in Spirit and he wanted to reconnect. What was his reality now? He tried to remember the love he had felt for him all those many years together. Love always overcame fear, he believed. Maybe this could be a key to helping Eric?

Because he was alone now and safe in his bed, without stranger's eyes watching him, concerned for his PTSD, he was going to face up to Eric. He breathed again and the smell became almost overpowering. It was blood, faeces, dust and gunpowder all mixed together in the stench of war.

Eric's eyes were watching him! He had been up front in the line of soldiers, clearing the area of IEDs as they walked gingerly across the last field before they got to the tree line. The enemy were close in and alert. The day was steamy hot and they were all pouring with sweat down their faces.

Eric had crouched down to examine something on the ground. He was doing the very responsible job which no-one envied him, but he was proving himself a reliable and good soldier and could take this extra stress.

An IED was there somewhere, it just needed locating! Very carefully he had felt around with his fingertips in the gravel on the track, and then it exploded, throwing him 20 feet in the air and taking off his legs and the lower half of his body.

Harry breathed again, the familiar panic gripping his gut. He was beginning to go out through the back of his head, like a steam train, joining Eric perhaps in the maelstrom of Energy which was Hell. He tried to get back, clutching with white fingers at the duvet cover. The cat suddenly leapt up onto his chest and started licking his face vigorously!

'Get off, you mad moggie,' he shouted, but laughed aloud as it brought him spinning back to reality.

Eric had gone again. He was at home in bed and very hungry! He got out of bed and went over to the mirror. The haunted look in his eyes was still there. He looked at himself long and hard and said,

'Harry, you are going to get better from this and get Annie back!' and he smiled at himself ruefully.

The shower was hot and he spent some time in it, lathering himself with the Lavender gel which Annie had bought him last birthday. The water was washing away the pain. He felt the fear spinning down the plughole, and Eric slipped by and hugged him briefly.

He remembered times when they used to shower together at Eric's house in Exmouth as boys, when his Mum had told them off for coming home covered in mud and sand, and had shooed them upstairs to clean off before tea. It was a lark being in the shower with someone else! Especially spraying each other with the hose up their noses, in their eyes and even up their bums! Molly, Eric's Mum, had scolded them, but laughingly too. She loved having two naughty boys in the house together!

The big fluffy towel which smelt of Annie was wrapped firmly round him as he went back to put on his jeans and Rugby shirt. He put some aftershave on his stubble and showed his short hair the brush, before going downstairs two at a time to get himself a large cooked breakfast.

Having been so very independent as a lad he was a good cook, and enjoyed pottering about in the kitchen when he was home. The bacon and eggs, with hash browns out of the freezer and some slightly shrivelled up mushrooms were nearly ready. He whistled softly to himself. It was nearly 11a.m.

Suddenly a huge booming sound shocked him into silence. He ran to the dining room and dived under the table, hiding his head in his arms, and panting loudly. He lay there for some minutes until his head cleared and he realised, of course it was November 11[Th] today and 11a.m. The troops would be lowering the flag and playing the last post. They had let off the big gun in remembrance. He should have been there with them.

He sat down at the table and put his first mouthful of bacon and egg into his mouth. He grinned. He was going to leave Lympstone and get a place somewhere quiet and start a new life with Annie. He hadn't a clue what he would do, but the first thing was to get out of this godforsaken institutional house, and find his own place to rent.

He switched on the TV and saw the Queen laying a wreath, recorded at last year's Cenotaph event, which would be repeated this Sunday. The British were so very good at this pomp and circumstance! All the soldiers in their shiny best would be marching past, pride in their hearts as they remembered the days of honour and glory in the last big war.

Then some of the current forces would troop by, many in wheelchairs with smashed limbs, eyes blown out, heads that were screwed up like his. He clenched his fists in anger.

'It's all such a bloody waste of time! It's f...ing madness. It's insanity worse than mine! It's costing the country £15 million a day to carry on this pantomime; and for what? It will go nowhere, and does nothing to keep providing the troops with more ammunition; and then training up more men to fight their own wars. It's just big business for the arms trade! No-one benefits! Innocent civilians are killed and maimed, people suffer extreme emotional damage, especially the kids, and the politicians get a buzz out of it, rather like school boys in the sand dunes. The soldier's lives are f...ked up, those that enjoy it are either morons or bullies or inadequate personalities. Heroes, my foot! They all go out there without a clue of what lies ahead, they hang in there together for security and when one of us gets blown to pieces it blows our marriages to pieces too! F..., f... f...! I'm out of it!'

Harry was shouting now, the sweat streaming down his face. His breakfast lay untouched as he screamed at the television. He got up and paced around the room. He would go straight across and sign off. His OC would see that he meant it! No more of the bloody tablets either. He was done with that. He would help himself from now on.

Annie's leaving him yesterday was the best thing that had happened to him. No longer was his rock there! He was just on his own now, able to make his own decisions; no one would feel sorry for him, or treat him with kid gloves, or even think of him as a hero. He was a stupid soldier and as such had learnt the hard way, which was all. He was getting out now!

He sat down again and wolfed down the remains of his breakfast, then slung the plate angrily into the sink. He grabbed his denim jacket and set off across the grass towards the office block. The sun was warm on his face and the birds were chirping almost as though it were the first day of spring. He stopped for a moment to calm his anger down. No point in upsetting the OC with a display of anger. He could be polite and to the point.

He gazed down across the river estuary, blue in the sunshine, and calm today. He would take a run along the cycle track once he had signed out, and then collect his stuff and go. Freedom at last! He had been in the Marines for 9 years and he would lose most of his pension rights but he didn't care a fig!

As he approached the office block he saw across the field the troops returning from the 11am minutes silence. He wasn't keen that any of them should see him dressed like this on a solemn day, so he ran the last few yards and headed up the stairs where Annie had climbed up only a couple of hours before.

He strode along the corridor, his military swagger still in evidence at such moments, his shoulders tight back, his arms swinging as though marching.

His heavy knock alerted the OC to his urgency.

'Come in,' he said quietly, wondering what the problem might be.

Harry scarcely altered his pace and marched straight up to the desk. He put his clenched fist on the big desk and looked intently at his commanding officer.

'I'm out. I'm off. I'm done with the Marines!'

The OC thought that Harry had had another brain storm and he gestured him to sit down on the big leather seat opposite him.

'Ok, mate! Not so fast! How are you feeling today? Has Annie been in touch?' he said, placating him.

'I'm fed up with this softly, softly approach. I'm going to quit. Annie has left me and I'm on my own now. I'm going to do my own thing and get myself out of this hell, but first I need to sign off.'

The OC took a sharp breath in. He wasn't sure he ought to let a man in his state just walk out. Perhaps he should call the medics to check him over first. He didn't want him doing anything silly which might reflect badly on the care he was given. He also realised that Harry meant what he said!

'Ok, let's have a chat about this. What are your plans?' he asked, playing for time. Perhaps Harry would crumple and go back to the house or could be persuaded to go into the infirmary here so they could assess him.

Harry looked straight at his commanding officer, who had seen him in such a state so many times over the last months. His voice was steady as was his gaze, as he looked intently across the desk.

'I know exactly what I'm doing, and I'm going to be fine. Eric has said that he'll help me, and I'm getting a place in Exmouth until I can sort out my marriage.'

The OC slowly took the papers from his filing cabinet and placed them carefully on the table in front of Harry.

'There's no going back once you've done it, you know,' he warned.

Harry scribbled his signature on the line that was indicated and breathed a sigh of relief as he did so. It was like coming to the end of a prison sentence; or signing out of slavery! Freedom at last!

He shook the OC's hand and listened half-heartedly to the information about winding up the accommodation and getting his kit checked out. He didn't really care now if his kit was just left in a dirty pile in the middle of the floor, and the keys left on the table. He had done with all the formality and regulations.

'Thanks for all your help, Sir,' he managed to say before turning on his heel and walking out of the office for ever.

Chapter 7

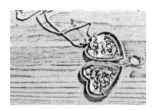

Harry walked quickly back to the house with a lightness in his step which he hadn't had for months. He automatically cleared the dishes and grabbed a few bits of food out of the fridge and freezer, putting them into a carrier bag, while he made a mental list of the bits he would take with him.

Upstairs he packed sparsely but with care, making sure that he left all traces of army life behind. He put his notebook and pen in and he took the locket from the dressing table which he had torn off yesterday in his grief, and now put it carefully back around his neck, giving it a gentle kiss as he did so. What would Annie be up to now? She was not due at work today, Friday. Perhaps he could try to ring her once he was out and about?

He didn't want her coming round here or trying to persuade him to go back on his decision. It would be tough financially for a while he realised, but once things were sorted he would get some benefits until he could find some sort of a job.

First things first though. He needed a bed for tonight. He would beg Molly, Eric's Mum, for a bit of sofa, till he could find a bedsit or flat.

As Molly still lived close to Annie's childhood home he would need to be careful that they didn't see him going in and out, but he wanted to have a catch up with her anyway. She needed the support as much as he did, and he had often felt inadequate to give that since Eric died.

He used his biggest kit bag for his bits and pieces. He would ditch that too once he had arrived somewhere. He wanted no reminders of his Marine days. He looked at the cat which was still curled up on the bed, and decided that only Amanda should know what had happened over these last two days. He needed to apologise to her anyway, he couldn't just leave things as they stood. Amanda must be feeling dreadful and she was such a nice girl too.

So he took out a piece of paper from the tatty bureaux and wrote in his scrawling hand;

Dear Amanda,
You've helped me so much, and I want you to forget what happened the other day.
Annie has gone to her parents and hasn't made contact yet. I've ditched out and will try to find a flat in Exmouth for the while.
Can you take the cat? Here are the keys if you want to help yourself to anything before they clear the house. Could you clear Annie's stuff too? I'm sure she'll be back to collect them.
Keep in touch,
Cheers
Harry XX

He pushed the note into a recycled envelop and would drop it through her letterbox on his way out.

Now he stood and looked around at what had been his, Annie's and Charlie's home for the last 9 years. He regretted uprooting Charlie, but soon he would be back on track and would be a proper father to him again. The house looked sad and dismissed, with things strewn haphazardly around, as he had sorted his stuff randomly.

Closing the door behind him, with his heavy rucksack on his back and just his denims and trainers on, he turned and walked briskly passed Amanda's door and down the track that led to the small gate which opened onto the river path. It wasn't used often and he would need to use the key he had been issued to get out. The barbed wire on the top of the gate looked menacing.

Once out, he flung the key back over the gate where it landed with a thud on the tarmac. There would be no going back now!

There was a light breeze blowing up the river from the sea, and the sun was peeping through. He was no longer as super fit as in earlier years so he walked rather than ran along the track, watching the sea and river birds at their daily business and seeing a few boats moored in the river. The tide was going out and the current was strong in places. A couple of sailing dinghies were cutting up the river, listing horribly in the wind.

It would take him about half an hour to reach Molly's place, so he got out his mobile and phoned her. As the phone rang, he felt Eric brush against him. He wasn't disturbed by this and just said,

'Yep, I'm out too now, mate! Wish me luck!'

The reeds by the river rustled to him in answer.

'Molly, it's Harry! Can I come by in a short while? I've ditched Lympstone and am walking to Exmouth!'

There was a brief pause before a warm smiley voice answered,

'Course you can, love! I'll get the kettle on! See you soon; that will be great.'

Chapter 8

Annie had slept very little that night. She lay awake worrying instead. She had spent too much of her meagre earnings on getting new stuff for Charlie and a few bits and pieces for herself. Exeter had been heaving with shoppers and her mother had got on her nerves. Being supportive was one thing, taking her over was quite another! She must watch that she didn't sink back into a sort of childhood state.

Her brain was still rather numb too and she kept getting a lump somewhere between her stomach and her throat which felt like lead. They had dropped into the insurance office on the way to shopping in Exeter and her boss had been most kind, to the point of bringing her close to tears again. She could take a few days as compassionate leave, or whatever they called it, and she should let them know when she would be back in, next week sometime, he'd said.

It was certainly a relief not to have to face the girls with all those questions but not having a routine and no home meant she was a bit at a loss, with not much to fill the long day.

She kept thinking of people she would like to phone and share her misery with, but then thought better of it, and remained just in the space of security that her mother was creating.

She had lots of friends, from school days in the town and also in the barracks, as she had joined the wives' choir some months back. They all got on really well together, working on music which was really challenging but also hugely enjoyable. But it didn't feel quite right to tell any of them about Harry and Amanda.

Everyone knew about Harry's PTSD and they were really supportive and sympathetic. But this was different. It was like washing your dirty linen in public and she didn't want to make things any harder for Harry than they already were.

She was sitting in the lounge watching daytime telly with her Dad. How unlike her that was! He often watched the football, but today for her sake they were looking at some inane programme about buying a property in Australia. She was almost dozing off.

Suddenly her iPhone rang. She had it on silent, but it vibrated in her jeans pocket, so she pulled it out to see who it was, feeling disinclined to answer. It was Amanda!

A dozen different emotions went through her like an electric shock; anger, disbelief, frustration, tinged with a longing to chat to her best friend about the whole situation. There might be some simple explanation?

She looked at the number as the phone continued to vibrate and finally pressed the answer button.

'Hi, is that you Annie? How are you doing? You must be so angry with me! Harry has ditched out and left the house! I hope he's ok? Will you come round so I can explain everything? The kids are off in nursery at the mo.'

She sounded so normal, and 'not guilty' that Annie answered cautiously,

'I'm at my Mum's. I'll come round if you really want me too. Harry can't have gone far.'

It was only 12.30 so without giving any explanation to her parents Annie shrugged into her woollen short jacket and grabbed her car keys and left the house, slamming the door.

Her parents looked at each other in amazement.

Annie drove automatically down the hill out of Exmouth and along the familiar road towards the barracks. She had not expected to be going back so soon. As she neared the entrance a feeling of dread and depression settled over her. She really didn't want to go back to that house. The shock of everything had given her thinking time too, and she realised that her life in the barracks was only half a life really. She had so much more in her to express, which could not be expressed within the confines of this huge institution, the Marines.

She drew up and parked outside Amanda's house, identical to hers, except for the pot of geraniums on the doorstep. Amanda was looking out for her and came straight to the door as she raised a hand to knock. Normally she would have walked straight in, but this wasn't 'normally'.

Amanda opened her arms to her and Annie, quite without thinking, rushed into them and started to sob like a child. Instead of feeling anger and hurt at what her friend had done, she was now getting support and love from her!

She was led into the lounge where music was playing and a candle burning in the cold grate. Amanda had already made the coffee and had put some rich custard creams out on a plate, which she now offered.

Once she was settled with a hot mug in her hands, Amanda handed Annie the letter she had found shoved through her letter box an hour earlier. Annie read it quickly and frowned.

'What the hell is going on?' she said breathlessly.

'I'm not sure but I think the shock of that slap may have something to do with it! He loves you Annie, and will do anything to make things right again. That day when you found us together in bed like that was just his request for some support. The stupid girl in the office had brought him home and dumped him alone to ruminate, and he rang me. He was in a bad way then and asked me if he could lie down. We weren't even undressed fully! I would NEVER, NEVER do anything like that, especially not with Harry. I love you both too much! You must trust me! Nothing happened, except what you saw. He must be feeling worse than me right now. I do hope he doesn't do anything stupid! Mind you, that note sounds quite focused and upbeat, don't you think?'

Annie couldn't answer. She was feeling too shocked and relieved to respond. Her worst fears had been brushed aside by Amanda's words. She should have listened to her own intuition rather than behaving like a frightened little girl. No wonder her mother was coddling her! Harry DID love her, of that she was sure. He needed her and had done since he was 15. He was now out there alone and very vulnerable. They must try to find him and get some sense into him.

Annie's practical side kicked in. Being an army girl she knew how to respond in a crisis (at least, usually) so now the first point of contact was her OC.

She picked up her phone and dialled the office number.

The OC answered straight away. She explained who she was and what she needed to know, in the matter-of-fact voice she used for work.

'You are correct that he has signed himself out of the barracks,' replied the OC. 'He walked in here this morning and signed out in a very calm and determined way. I suspect he may be heading for Exmouth as I saw him walking cross the yard in that direction with a large backpack. Good luck to you both. Oh, and Mrs Kenny, when you have cleared your stuff could you please come and sign the final papers and drop in the keys, thank you.'

Annie turned off her phone and looked across at her friend who was waiting expectantly.

'Well, it looks as though we really *are* homeless now! He's signed out and was last seen heading for Exmouth. I suspect he may have gone down to Molly's where he'll feel safe. I hope so anyway. That's the end of an era for us!'

'I shall be losing some very dear friends,' said Amanda, very close to tears herself now. 'I do wish you could have stayed till Rod got back. I shall miss you so much.'

One of the characteristics of army life is its transience and they both knew that. You never knew who you would be working with, or posted with, or even have to share a tent with. But once families came along, the wives try to stick together for support at least.

'My first job is to rescue some stuff before the 'Powers that be' put it all in the skip', laughed Annie. 'I suppose some of that furniture is worth saving, though it's all rather tired. We're not going to have pennies to throw around now, that's a cert! I'll have to find a firm to store it for us until we can get sorted out.'

She jumped off the sofa, now in action mode and grabbed Amanda's Yellow Pages which were lying on the side table. Scrabbling through the section on removals she got a pen and marked a couple of numbers before rapidly dialling on her phone. Amanda looked on rather bemused. This was all happening so fast. What would life be like without her best friend just across the road?

'Will you come across with me? I don't fancy going into that hole alone now after what happened. I'll get some stuff loaded into the car that we need now. The firm are bringing boxes with them and will pack the china at least,' she went on. 'They can be here at 8a.m tomorrow.'

'Crumbs! That was quick work! I'll have to pick up the girls soon from nursery. I'll come across with you, and then go straight on for them. Come in and have some lunch with us when you're ready.'

So Annie and Amanda went across to the empty house and cautiously opened the door, not sure of what they would find. The lounge had stuff strewn around as though someone had left in a hurry and upstairs was even worse. A pile of dirty washing was on the bedroom floor and the fridge door had been left open. The cat ran downstairs to greet them, obviously expecting some breakfast.

'Oh, men! They never change!' moaned Annie, as she got out a roll of black sacks and started to sort the dirty clothes into piles. She got a fair bit of stuff from Charlie's room, remembering his school book and his favourite toys, and some play clothes, and then got a suitcase from under her bed, dusted it off and filled it with her clothes and bits of make-up. These things she loaded into her small car until the back was piled to the roof.

Downstairs Amanda was busy emptying the fridge and freezer, cleaning it out and doing the dishes. She checked the cupboards for perishables and put everything into a couple of large canvas shopping bags she found. She fed the cat too, who was winding around her legs, looking for attention. Eventually she picked it up and stroked its glossy neck.

'Oh, Moggy, you'll have to keep me company now. I need someone to talk to in the evenings, or I'll go mad.' The cat just continued purring, so she put it down and it ran over to its bowl of fresh food and started eating hungrily.

She then checked her watch and shouted up to Annie that she *had* to go or the kids would be kept waiting.

'I'll be over in the morning to give you a hand to clean up, once I've dropped them off at nursery,' she yelled.

Annie stood on the landing alone once the door had slammed shut and took a deep breath. This was all happening so fast! She hadn't a chance to think about anything. She was worried about Harry, but couldn't get round to ringing him till she'd cleared a bit more stuff. Their home of the last 9 years was disappearing in front of her eyes. Where would she end up next and would Harry be with her? The prospect of staying any length of time at her parents was unthinkable. She could imagine all sorts of scenarios with and without Harry, but not with her parents!

Finally everything was gone through and she knew what would be going into storage tomorrow when the removal men came. She glanced around again to check everything and then turned off the gas, water and electric and took the final readings, before going over to the office once more to see the OC.

It was quiet in the building as most people were at lunch, but she had rung over to say she was on her way. The big familiar desk was tidy and had just one form on it, the one which would sign them out for ever. The OC went through it, and agreed that she could bring in the keys once the van was loaded up tomorrow.

'We will miss you, Mrs Kenny' he said in a kindly way. 'I do hope that Harry makes a good fresh start, he deserves to do well. I'm sure the symptoms will gradually lessen.'

Annie just smiled back at him as she signed the form. She couldn't bring herself to speak as she was feeling so full of anger at the Military Establishment, and all the waste and carnage which it generated. She knew she would never have any more to do with them. These people were so institutionalised that they had no concept of any other life, a normal life which she was now longing for. She turned her back and walked out with her head held high and her heart pounding with joy at the prospect of leaving the barracks for ever.

Back in her noisy kitchen Amanda had prepared a big pot of pasta, with special tasty meat sauce, a favourite with the girls and they were waiting for Annie as she walked back into their cosy home for the last time.

'Annie, sit by me,' shrieked Miranda, the 3 year old, as she came in. So she did, and the meal was jolly and chaotic as usual. They polished it off with another mug of coffee and some Ferrero Rocher chocolates which Amanda had found in the cupboard.

'My parents will have a nice shock when I get back! I didn't want to ring them though, as Mum would be over to 'help' like a shot!'

'When are you going to ring Harry then?' said Amanda gently. She had been expecting her friend to do so all morning and she still hadn't.

Annie smiled wryly.

'I'm not going to!' she announced, 'Harry needs to know that he hurt me, and has destroyed everything we have built up together! He can phone me; when he's ready,' she said firmly.

Amanda gave her best friend a big hug.

'Well done you!' she said.

Chapter 9

After wishing her friend and the girls a fond farewell, Annie headed back towards her parent's house with the car loaded up to the roof with her stuff. She didn't drive directly to them though, but veered off into the town centre and parked up near the leisure centre, putting an hour onto the parking ticket.

She walked briskly through the shopping mall towards the Strand, where she knew there was an estate agent that did rentals. She was just going to 'smell out the market' and see if there was anything which might suit her and Charlie for a while. 6 months rental would give her time to sort out her feelings about Harry and enable her to take stock.

Exmouth was a handy location generally as her parents would be willing to babysit whenever she needed them, and close enough to Exeter to still keep her job down. She wondered if she could pick up some extra hours at the office now, as she would need more income because she was on her own.

This prospect did not faze her right now. She felt inwardly calm and in action mode and knew that Charlie would be ok so long as she was.

She scanned the window with its neat pictures and descriptions of rental properties. Wow, she hadn't realised how prices had gone up. There wasn't anything under £500 a month, and that was fairly pokey.

She tentatively pushed open the door and walked across to the young lady with blond hair who was scanning her computer.

'Good afternoon,' she started, to get her attention. The girl looked up with a bored expression and flicked her long hair. She could have been attractive with a less sour face, thought Annie.

'I'm looking for a cheap flat for me and my son of 7,' she went on. 'I can't afford very much, as I've just left the Barracks and I'm on my own.'

At the mention of the Marines, the girl looked at her keenly. Was this woman a war widow? She would have to treat her kindly. But she hadn't much to offer her. She went over to the filing cabinet and flicked through a few properties, and then she picked out a couple and laid them on the desk.

'What about these?' she said in a friendly way.

The two flats were both near the town centre, but in side streets so not too noisy. They had only one bedroom though, and Charlie would miss his play space. Maybe she could sleep on a sofa in the lounge and let him have the bedroom? It wasn't ideal by any means, but beggars can't be choosers, so she asked if she could see them both tomorrow, her day off, after the removal men had cleared their house, in the early morning.

Both properties were furnished, so she wouldn't need to sort anything out from what she had left in the house now. It could all just go into storage.

She took the details and walked back to the car with a spring in her step. At least there was something on the horizon now to explore. She could go back to her parents and state her intentions without becoming bamboozled by her bossy mother.

Glancing at her watch she saw it was already school pickup time, so she headed for the playground entrance and met Charlie with a big smile and a hug.

'How about going for a swim, then some chips after?' she suggested. Charlie grinned. His swimming lessons had finished last term, but he really enjoyed going in with his Mum and having a good splash and game. He could swim a whole width now too.

He went to get into the back of the car, and then stopped in amazement. The back seat was completely full of boxes and bags!

'You'll have to be in front just until we get to Gran's. I've been to get some of your toys from home.' Annie explained.

Completely accepting of this explanation, Charlie jumped into the front seat and they were soon at the leisure centre car park again.

The swim did them both good. Annie swam a few lengths too and felt some of the tension easing out of her tired limbs. She had done a lot of humping and lifting this morning. They laughed a lot together and that was always good for stress.

Once they were changed, with wet hair still dripping, they went to the café and ordered chips and a mug of tea for Annie and special hot chocolate for Charlie. They sat opposite each other and then Annie said,

'I've got something important to tell you, Love. Dad and I are splitting up; and you and I are going to live in a flat in Exmouth for a while. All our big stuff is going into a storage place tomorrow and we won't be going back home again. Dad will see you sometimes, I'm sure!'

This last sentence was added as a half lie, as she hadn't a clue even where Harry was. But she was sure he would want to see Charlie, just as soon as he had got his act together. She felt angry that he still hadn't rung her about his plans. She had just been left with all the clearing up to do! She was worried too, in case he had done something stupid in his present mental state.

But none of this was she going to show to Charlie. He was looking at her now with his big eyes. He would accept things if she was upbeat.

'But I thought we were going to live with Gran and Grampi!' was all he said.

'Well, we could, but Gran is getting older and doesn't want all our noise and chaos around her all the time,' she tried to explain lamely.

It was hard talking to the child as she never told him lies, but she had done so twice in 5 minutes. She would have to apologise to him and explain properly, once they were settled in their own place and things were clearer.

'Let's go and tell Gran now shall we?' she suggested.

Chapter 10

Stella was biting her lip so hard that it was nearly bleeding. The last thing in the world she wanted was to fall out with her only child, especially when Annie was so vulnerable and stressed. She was sensitive enough to realise that this rejection of her help and home was just Annie's way of getting through this trauma. She also understood, as only the wiser older generation can, just how much stress Annie had had to cope with since she had left school and gone to live at the Barracks.

She and Ted had been really pleased to welcome her back home, but as a grown married woman with a child, things were very different and she understood that probably Annie was better off in her own space. But Annie hadn't taken 5 minutes to organise everything! No sooner had Stella got them set up in her home than they were talking of leaving them again!

Charlie was now in bed, happy with a pile of his favourite toys strewn across the little bedroom floor. He had hugged his Grampi hard as Annie was explaining about the removal van and the new flat she was going to look at in the morning. Grampi was upset and needed comfort, of that he was sure! It also made him feel less scared hugging his best Grampi! Where would his next bed be in a few days' time?

Annie had managed to stay calm and focused as she talked. She also didn't want to upset her parents, who were her mainstay now she was on her own. They certainly had been very supportive over the last years and especially since Harry had been sent back to Lympstone after Eric's death. That was more than a year ago now and it had been the toughest year of her life.

Her parents, as well as caring devotedly for Charlie whenever she asked, had also listened to her side of the story and kept their criticism of the war to themselves. She knew that her Dad thought they should never have gone into Afghanistan in the first place, but they had never discussed it openly together.

They sat now by the little coal fire in the sitting room and were watching Stella's favourite soap, 'Emmerdale', which couldn't be missed! Annie was dead tired. She had unpacked a few bits and pieces for Charlie and made space for him to sit in the back of the car; her brain kept jumping hither and thither remembering things she needed to get from the house in the morning, before it all disappeared into the back of the lorry.

'I'm off to bed,' she said quietly. 'Got a long day tomorrow! Good night!' Stella gave her a hug; there were no ill feelings.

Once upstairs Annie got out her mobile phone and checked it for a message from Harry. Still nothing! She felt tempted to ring him, despite all her good resolve. She was missing him so much; there was a sort of ache in her gut, which wrenched every time she thought of him. Was he still alive? Had he gone to Eric's Mum, Molly? That was the most obvious place of refuge.

Her fingers hovered above the keys, ready to dial the familiar number. Just then her phone rang. She jumped at the sudden noise and vibration in her hand! It was Amanda!

'Hi, I just wanted to check you were alright,' said her friend. 'No word from Harry yet?'

'No, and I haven't rung him either, although I've felt tempted. Tomorrow I'm going to look at a couple of flats in town after the removal men have finished. Want to come?'

Amanda was keen, she liked exploring new properties, and it made a change from looking out of the window at the Barracks. The girls would be at nursery anyway.

'I'll come across and give you a hand with the clean up too, after the men leave; I'll bring my Henry,' Amanda went on.

'You're a star!' said Annie and hung up. She would sleep better now knowing she wouldn't have to do that last bit on her own. The house held so many bad memories and was so spooky at times. She would be really glad to be out of it.

She was also looking forward to seeing the two flats. She got into bed and reread the details of them both trying to imagine herself in them. One had a nice new kitchen; that would be a novelty after the tatty Barracks one! The other one had 'sea glimpses' whatever that meant.

With a smile of gratitude on her face she snuggled down. She had friends, parents and a wonderful son, and she was about to launch out on her own new adventure.

Chapter 11

Annie woke up early and wondered where she was. The familiar bedroom at the barracks had faced east and normally the early sun woke them. At her parents' house it faced north-west and it was still dark anyway.

Gradually it dawned on her that today was the big move out of her old life into her new one. What would she find and would she manage on her own? It felt pretty scary, as she had never lived on her own before or been totally responsible for bills and decisions. Even when Harry was poorly, as he so often was, the barracks had been like a protective shield around them, and 'real life' had hardly existed.

Now she carefully dressed in her best slacks and jacket which she used for interviews and formal occasions. She wanted to look her best for the viewings. Then she suddenly remembered that she had to clean up the old house first, which might be mucky, so she slid back into her old jeans and jumper and put the jacket on a hanger to take with her. She felt jumpy and tired after a broken night.

After she had taken Charlie to school and promised to pick him up in good time, as he too was a bit clingy, she turned her attention to the barracks. This was the final time she would have to enter those gates and show her pass to the soldier on duty. He saluted her casually and she drove down to her old house, one of a grey row looking out towards the river.

The removal van was already parked up outside. The 3 men were having a quick fag and reading the Sun up in the cab. When they saw her unlocking the front door they slid down and greeted her affably.

'We'll start with the kitchen packing, miss!'

Annie charged around gathering a few bits and bobs into a big holdall, and tried to show the men what was what. It was all falling into chaos and she felt her stress levels rising. Soon cupboards, beds and chairs were being safely stowed away into the huge van; her home was disappearing in front of her eyes. When would she see this lot again, and would Harry be sharing it with her?

She sat down on the kitchen stool which was still lingering sadly amongst the boxes. The men were doing a good job packing all their kitchen stuff and china. She hadn't organised tea for them either!

Just then Amanda waltzed in, carrying a tray with 5 steaming mugs of strong tea, some sugar in a bag, and 5 big doughnuts oozing with red jam.

'Here you are everyone!' she announced proudly. 'I knew you wouldn't have anything to refresh the inner man!'

Annie smiled at her wanly and took a big bite of a warm doughnut, leaving jam and sugar all around her mouth. She glanced at her watch. It was already 11.15 and the men were having their first fag break. At this rate they wouldn't be finished until this afternoon. What about the flat viewings? She was due at the estate agents at midday.

'We should be done in half an hour,' said the biggest chap, who was obviously in charge. 'We're done upstairs and there are only a few more bits to go in down here!'

Annie was astounded and wandered in a total daze up the stairs to view the empty rooms. Amanda was just behind her.

'I'll pop home and get Henry, and then we can do upstairs while they're finishing down in the kitchen,' she said in a practical way.

Soon the top floor was clean and cleared of all rubbish and Annie and Amanda were tackling the lounge. It echoed strangely without the furniture, and suddenly Annie had an image of Eric in front of her. He was looking at her with bloodshot accusing eyes. Then the image disappeared as fast as it had come.

Annie shook her head, too scared to speak, and just looked at the place where Eric had been. She rushed across to Amanda and hugged her.

'I've just seen Eric.' She breathed into Amanda's shoulder. 'No wonder Harry freaks out when that happens. This place is haunted, Manda!'

Her friend held her tight and then said,

'Well, you'll soon be out of here for good!'

True to their word, the men had finished very soon and Annie took the keys up to the office. Just in time to get to the estate agents too! The door finally slammed shut and her back to her past traumas, Annie felt a surge of energy as she drove with her friend towards the town.

The first flat was in a quiet side street near the shops; up an outside staircase and straight into the lounge. It was nice and bright and newly furnished in pale beige colours, with a good size bedroom for Charlie and the sofa bed for her. She liked its airiness and convenience to the centre. Amanda thought it was great too and immediately was imagining plants on the window sill, a cat to use the cat flap and some pictures on the walls, as well as candles and incense for good measure!

'Do you want to see the other one for comparison?' she asked.

Annie thought for a moment, and then turned to the young lady who was showing them around.

'How soon could I move in here?' she enquired.

'Well, as you are coming from the Barracks we can jump the queue in taking up references. Maybe next Monday would be possible. I'll check with the landlord for you.'

She took out her mobile phone and rapidly dialled a number.

A quick conversation assured them of a guaranteed start to a six month lease by next Monday.

'Ok, I'll take it then,' said Annie, relieved that it was all so easy.

'You can pick up the keys at 9.30 next Monday,' smiled the young lady.

Amanda gave her a big hug.

'This needs a celebration,' she said as she led a bemused Annie back to the car.

Some while later they were sitting on the balcony of their favourite seafront pub, sipping their glasses of cool lager. They had ordered some potato wedges with dipping sauce to go with it, and they both took a deep breath.

'Well here's to your new start,' said Amanda and raised her glass.

Chapter 12

Meanwhile Harry was starting out on his own adventure. After leaving the Barracks he walked rapidly towards Molly's house, never looking back or pausing. His mind felt pleasantly relaxed today after his long sleep and his anger blow-out earlier. He must have released a lot of tension, he thought to himself.

He felt enormous relief at leaving Lympstone too, and wondered why he hadn't made this break earlier. He supposed that it was about courage; courage to stand on his own two feet again.

His feelings turned to Annie, whom he loved so very much. It began to dawn on him a little just how selfish he had been over the last months, wallowing in his own traumas and relying on her totally for his very existence. He began to see his behaviour through her eyes; his moodiness, his demands for peace and quiet at times when she would perhaps have liked to make love, or go out dancing. He had really become a boring old fart!

He hadn't been a very good father to Charlie either. Often he had ignored his requests for a game or a story, humping his shoulders and remaining silent. What child deserved behaviour like that, especially his own dear Charlie? He was such a loving lad and had often just come over quietly and sat beside him when he was feeling panicky or depressed.

As he walked and these thoughts became clearer, Harry started to feel more and more guilty and ashamed of the person he had become over the last year. The slap on his cheek had certainly been a wake-up call. How could he have treated Annie like that, and given her such a shock? Now she was at her parent's house which he knew wouldn't be easy for either of them. He must give her some time to forgive him and let her anger ease before he made contact. He couldn't bear to think of her hating him, or not wanting to see him. He would give it a few days, maybe a week, before he rang her. By then she would have calmed down again and would be willing to talk it over, he was sure.

Harry paused briefly and gazed down the river towards the sea. He had always loved the sea and felt good by it. In the Barracks they rarely had the chance to wander beside it. Now he breathed deeply and the salty tang hit his nostrils. The cool November day was beautiful he thought, as he watched the black headed gulls circling and dipping over the water. A small sailing boat was heading towards the shore near him and he saw a single man handling the ropes leaning out against the wind.

'I fancy doing that!' he murmured to himself. There were so many aspects of life to explore now that he had freedom. He knew that money would be tight at first but his heart leapt at the thought of new hobbies and travel with Annie and Charlie. Perhaps they could get a small boat to enjoy together?

He smiled to himself, and realised what an unfamiliar feeling it was. His muscles weren't used to doing it anymore! Heading towards the town he cut through the alleyway towards Molly's house. He mustn't linger as she was expecting him.

Molly had become like his surrogate Mum during his teenage years. Because his parents had split up, he rarely saw his own Mum, and his Dad was involved in work and chasing new ladies. Eventually he had met someone who suited him better, but she was a bossy bitch and didn't want Harry in their lives, so he had spent more and more time out of the house, around at Eric's, or at Annie's, once they had started dating.

He hadn't really seen Molly since the funeral. She had rung a couple of times soon afterwards, obviously wanting some support, but he had been insensitive to this, being in his own dark hole of grief and terror. Now he felt another pang of guilt as this realisation began to dawn on him. He must make it up to her somehow in the next weeks.

He rang the doorbell, feeling a little nervous for the first time. He need not have worried as the door was flung open and warm arms were thrown around him. The familiar smell and ample breasts made him feel like a child again and he was close to tears as she pulled him away and looked him up and down.

'Well, Harry! I would have known you anywhere,' was all she said now; but privately she saw the dark rings under his eyes and the haunted look which still lingered. His hair had receded too and the dark stubble on his chin made him look older. She could have taken him for 35 rather than 27.

Harry observed her too. She was a buxom woman, quite handsome in a way, and had thick hair which waved around her face. Now it had turned steely grey and added years to her appearance. Grief and pain had chizzled lines into her face too and her blue/grey eyes looked strained, although right now they were smiling down at him.

'Come in, won't you,' she teased, taking his pack from him. 'Hey, that weighs a lot, have you come for a month?'

He didn't answer. There was enough time to explain everything once they were sitting down cosily in the kitchen. They always sat at the table and chatted rather than going into the small lounge with its slightly dated furniture. She had china dogs on the mantelpiece and dried flowers in vases on the window sill. It was a very 'mumsy' room he always thought. But then Molly was in her early 60s. She had always been ageless to him though.

The kettle was humming on the gas stove and Molly quickly made the tea in the old brown pot which had always been there. The mugs were the same too. He always had one with a picture of a classic car on it which she thought he would like. The dark brown liquid was comforting and gave them a familiar feel of friendship.

They took a few sips silently warming their hands before Molly said,

'Well, what's going on then?'

She knew him well enough to know that he was in some crisis, but not having seen him for 18 months she couldn't quite sort out what was happening.

Harry took a deep breath and started to tell her everything. At first it came out slowly and rather jumbled, but as he recounted the traumas of the last year, and then what had happened in the last two days, she listened more and more intently.

'And now I'm homeless and haven't made contact with Annie either. But I'm going to get better, of that I'm certain,' he ended lamely.

Molly put her mug down slowly on the kitchen table and looked across at this lad who had known her dear son so well, and had become almost like a son to her himself.

'You're welcome to stay in the lounge as long as you need to. This will always be a place you can call home.'

They both had tears in their eyes as they went through to the lounge. On a side table Molly had set up a memorial to her son Eric. There was a smiling picture of him in uniform, looking young and handsome as he was before they set out for Afghanistan. There was a medal which had been presented to her for his work with IEDs, for bravery. There were a couple of photos of him as a boy, one taken out on the sand-dunes with Harry at about the age of 11. There was a bunch of red carnations which Molly always kept topped up and fresh. And there was his cap, grubby and worn but still intact after the explosion. She had been presented with it at the funeral.

They stood side by side holding hands, looking down at the picture. Eric came and stood beside them too. He was calmer now and happy that Molly and Harry were together again at last.

'Healing takes its time,' said Molly wisely.

Chapter 13

Harry wondered where the days were going. Having arrived into the warm environment of Molly's home he started to relax more than he had done in years, and he slept and slept. His bed on the sofa was adequate and he had got a sleeping bag and a cushion. Every night he slept for at least 10 hours. He woke in the mornings and made a light breakfast for himself and Molly, then read the paper or watched some TV, and then went back to bed for another sleep.

Sometimes he got out his notebook and reread what he had written so far and he often just sat and looked at the picture of Eric, who smiled back at him and calmed his shattered nerves. Eric was closer than ever now, but never appeared in his blooded and torn state, with his wild accusing eyes. Instead he was more like a warm presence with them both whenever they shared memories of him. Molly was less aware of this presence than Harry, but she too seemed to be receiving comfort and was working through some of her grief to a place of acceptance.

Harry still hadn't rung Annie. The days were going by and it was now nearly a week since that fatal slap. His mobile hadn't rung either. What was she up to, and was she ok at her parents, he often wondered?

One sunny afternoon his sleepiness seemed to lift and a spark of energy was there. He decided to go for a run along the beach, so getting his denim jacket and trainers on, he left the house and darted down along the alley out of sight of Annie's parents' house and down to the docks, and so onto the beach. The kids weren't out of school yet and there were only a few dog walkers out on the sand. The tide was out, leaving a stretch of firm sand along the water's edge, covered in places by fine shells. It was ideal for a run and he set off, gently at first, feeling his limbs heavy after so much rest and sleep.

He must get himself fit again if he was to recover fully! The air in his lungs was cold and hurt him but he continued steadily, until the adrenalin rush of a good run started to kick in. Taking long strides, he increased his pace, until he was speeding along beside the sand dunes and approaching the red cliffs at the end of the beach. He was taking the same route that Annie had done the week before. He found the self-same rock on the long beach of Sandy Bay where she had sat and rested, looking out to sea. He wanted to phone Annie then as he felt her presence so close, but he had come without his mobile! He would do it later when he got back to Molly's.

Heading back the same way, but a bit slower now, his legs felt good and achy too after their first run in over a year. Sweat was dripping off his nose and his t-shirt was clinging to his back. He veered up off the beach to the promenade and came to a halt outside the Old Railway Carriage tearoom. He would stop there. He had some loose change in his denim jacket, enough for a coffee. An intense feeling of pleasure washed over him, at the prospect of sitting in a café alone for as long as he liked.

The Old Railway Carriage was literally what it said, an old carriage which had been brought here by some enterprising person and done up as a simple café.

On this November afternoon there were few people about, and there was only one other person in the café. Harry ordered a black coffee and sat down half way down the carriage, facing the other man who was reading a book.

He was slim, with his greying hair tied back in a ponytail. He was wearing a woollen patterned top, the kind that one finds at folk festivals, made in South America. He wore round gold-rimmed specs, which made him look like an ageing hippy. Harry, who enjoyed people-watching, gazed at him in an interested way. The man looked up after a few moments and smiled warmly at him.

'It's nice and peaceful here isn't it? You are looking for Peace.'

Harry wasn't sure how to respond. The man had told the truth with such calm assurance it was rather unnerving.

'I'm Gerry, by the way,' he continued. 'The young man with you right now is longing for freedom too. He's attached himself to you since his trauma.'

The man was gazing above Harry's left shoulder with wide grey eyes. Harry felt very uncomfortable but at the same time he trusted this man and what he was saying.

'Come and sit by me so we can talk,' Gerry was now saying. Harry moved over and sat opposite the stranger. He was eager to find out more, especially as Gerry was so gentle and non-invasive. Maybe he could help him with his PTSD? He seemed to know what he was talking about. Harry didn't normally talk to strangers about his thoughts and feelings, he was quite a private man usually, but since all these things had happened recently nothing was 'usual' any more. He now felt compelled to share his story with him.

'I've just left the Marines,' started Harry tentatively. 'I've been suffering from post-traumatic stress since my friend Eric was blown up by an IED in Afghanistan. I spent a bit of time in the luney bin, but recently have been struggling to hold down an office job in Lympstone Barracks. My wife has just left me because she found me in bed with her best friend. It was nothing at all. I ditched out of the Marines a few days ago and now I'm staying with Eric's Mum in town and have no idea what to do next.'

Stated like this it sounded a bit melodramatic to Harry's ears, but Gerry listened calmly and nodded.

'It's Eric who is with you still. I'm a psychic healer and could try and help you both if you wanted. Eric needs to move on and you need to get yourself well again. That's for Annie and Charlie's sake too!'

How did this man know their names? Harry hadn't mentioned them! He *must* be psychic! Harry had never had anything to do with this sort of thing before. Annie had once gone to the Spiritualist Church but he had thought her crazy at the time and hadn't understood it at all. Goose pimples started to break out all over him.

'Here is my card. If you feel like giving me a ring sometime we could make an appointment for you to come and have a healing session. I accept just donations, if finances are tight.'

There it was; an offer of help, no pressure, no adverts, no hype; just a simple card with his name and phone number on it. Harry felt slightly dizzy as he took the card from Gerry.

'I'll ring you tomorrow if I may,' he said slightly breathlessly. He needed a night to think it over. He didn't want any hocus-pocus or weirdoes interfering in his life. But he was at a crossroads and maybe this had come just at the right time. He shook Gerry's hand, drained his cup rapidly and walked down the steps out of the Railway Carriage. It was already getting dusky as he made his way back through town to Molly's place. He needed a good shower after his run and he was ravenously hungry now.

As he opened the front door a wonderful smell of mutton and barley stew met his nostrils. Molly knew it was his favourite dish. She used to make it for them back in the old days when he and Eric came in from rugby practice. He pulled off his sandy trainers and washed his hands. Going into the kitchen he put his arm around his favourite 'Mum'. It was so good to have a bit of normal home life again.

'I'll just pop up and shower, as I've been out running,' he said.

'That's a good sign!' remarked Molly. She knew the rest and exercise would do its work in his recovery. 'See you soon, as it's nearly ready!'

Up in the shower, with the hot water falling all around him, Harry had the chance to think about his encounter with Gerry. He seemed genuine enough and going by his 'gut instinct' Harry felt inclined to try and make an appointment for some healing. He always trusted his gut instinct. It had got him out of some close shaves in Afghanistan and enabled him to stay alive a couple of times. He didn't know much about psychics or healing but he knew from his own experiences that there was something more than what the eye could see. His experiences with Eric had proved that.

In the Psychiatric Hospital, where they took him after he had 'lost himself' completely, they tried to deaden everything that was happening to him with drugs. They had used some pretty strong ones, he knew that, but with little affect. All they seemed to do was make him feel totally exhausted and lousy and 'spaced out'; but Eric had still been there! The psychiatrist had told him it was a form of schizophrenia and that he would need to take tablets for the rest of his life. That was a joke! How little they knew and understood in the world of mental illness. They had tried to give him ECT too, but Annie had refused to sign the consent form having seen the film 'One flew over the cuckoo's nest'. You never knew how that sort of treatment would leave you. Sometimes not much better than a cabbage!

As he showered and these thoughts were spinning through his head, he realised how lucky he had been to have the love and support of his good wife. However long it was going to take, he wanted to try and heal himself as naturally as possible and go along with what Annie believed; that the body knows best.

He rubbed himself dry, feeling really good after his run, and went down to Molly smelling of soap and with wet touselled hair. She looked up from serving him a big plateful of stew and laughed.

'That's better. You look ten years younger already

87

Chapter 14

That evening after supper Harry decided to ring Annie. He took a deep breath before dialling the familiar number. It rang a couple of times before her light voice answered. Charlie would be in bed by now he knew, so they could talk uninterrupted.

'Hello, Harry! Where are you? Is everything OK?'

She sounded tense and concerned. The last thing he wanted was her fussing over him. He needed to be his own boss for a while and not have her always watching him for symptoms and asking if he was ok! He suddenly realised how their relationship had changed since he had got back. She had become his carer really, no longer his wife!

'Yep, I'm fine!' he answered casually, avoiding the questions. 'How is Charlie doing?'

Annie realised that he was playing hard to catch, and answered in a stilted way also,

'Oh, he's fine too. We're living in a flat now,' she added as an afterthought. He would have to know sometime anyway if he was ever going to see Charlie.

Harry took a gulp. This was a completely new scenario which he hadn't anticipated. She had gone and got herself somewhere to live, on her own with Charlie, away from her parents. That meant she had taken on a 6 month lease and intended to go it alone!

'I'm staying with Molly for the while,' he retorted, slightly defensively too. If she could do it, so could he! It wouldn't make it any easier to come back together if she was going it alone in a flat. He usually got on well with her parents and had anticipated that they would help him sort out this quarrel somehow. Now it was looking a bit bleak! He felt his stress level rising and the shake which always came with it started in his legs, and began to rise towards his gut.

'I'll speak soon,' was all he managed to say before cutting her off.

He sat on the sofa, feeling sick and the whirring noise started in his head. He was going to flip out if he wasn't careful. Black spots started appearing in front of his eyes and the smell and noise of gunfire started to come in.

'Oh f...k!' was all he managed to say, before he took a nose dive into Hell.

Just then Molly came into the lounge, carrying two cups of coffee. She had never experience anyone like this and took one look at him, curled up on top of his sleeping bag, his eyes staring straight ahead.

'Hey, Harry! What's up? Can you take this cup of coffee before I spill it?'

She remained calm and practical and her voice echoed in his head. Gradually the whirring stopped and Harry lifted his head. She was standing over him, the coffee cup poised just above him.

'Oh, sorry Molly,' he spluttered, coming to.

'You scared me for a moment,' she said.

Harry realised that in order for this not to happen again he would have to share some of his nightmares with her. So they sat side by side and talked long into the night. He tried to explain what happened in these moments of panic and how he seemed to flip out and only get the noise and smell of war.

She told him about Eric's childhood dream of being a soldier, and how he wanted to really help people out there. How proud she was that he had started clearing the IEDs as a job, rather than killing people and how she would always think of him as a hero.

Harry also started telling her a bit about life in Camp Bastion, how hot, dusty and difficult it had been; how the squadron had stuck together and the friendships which had formed there.

'Have you seen any of them since?' she enquired.

Harry realised that he hadn't. He had been so self-engrossed it hadn't occurred to him to try and make contact with any of his mates. It had all been between him and Eric for months and months. He began to see his illness from the outside and realise that he was not the only soldier in the world to come back damaged by the experience. Maybe some of his mates from those times would appreciate a call too?

Then their conversation turned to the here and now. How was he going to get Annie back? He realised now just how much he had hurt her; how she must have packed up the house on her own and then gone and found herself a flat. She had more courage than he had!

Molly, as ever practical and motherly suggested,

'Why don't you write her a letter rather than phoning her again? You could at least apologise for what happened and suggest you get together with Charlie. Her feelings have obviously been really hurt and the only person that can make them better is you!'

She hadn't actually blamed him, but made it clear in her blunt way that *he* could start the reconciliation. He felt slightly told off, but took it like a man!

'Ok! Maybe I should send the letter to her parents, as she didn't give me her address. I suppose Amanda has been in touch with her too? Maybe she could help smooth the troubled waters a bit, if I rang her?'

As it was already very late he hugged Molly good night and then crashed out again on the sofa. There were plenty of things to focus on tomorrow morning, the first one being to ring Gerry and get an appointment to visit him.

Chapter 15

The very first thought to come into Harry's head next morning was Gerry. He had been having a strange dream. He was sitting on a bench in Phear Park with Eric as boys and they were chatting happily together. Gerry had walked over towards him, holding out both his hands. As he got to them Eric had turned to Harry and kissed him goodbye, then got up and walked away, into a sort of light tunnel, which he couldn't see the end of. It had left Harry feeling sad but peaceful, and as he woke he wiped a real tear from his eye.

He lay for a few moments remembering the dream, and wondering if he had been shown something true. He had read about tunnels of light when people died, but he didn't really understand it at all. The feeling of peace was real though and he was smiling as he went through to join Molly. The sun was just up and filtering across the kitchen.

'It's going to be another nice day,' he remarked. 'I'm going out for a bit.'

Molly looked at him quizzically and pointed to a writing pad, biro and envelopes which she had found in the bureaux for him.

'Aren't you going to write to your wife first?' she asked.

Slightly reprimanded by her comment, he looked down at the paper on the table. He hated writing letters at the best of times, but knew this one had to be done.

'I'll tackle it later when I've had some fresh air,' he replied, not mentioning his dream or his burning need to see Gerry. He hadn't told her about his encounter yesterday in the Railway Carriage either.

Taking his mobile in his jacket pocket, which also still had Gerry's card tucked safely away, he walked briskly down to the sea front. Taking big gulps of sea air, he walked along till he got to the gardens by the Pavilion. Here he stopped and found a bench.

His fingers shook as he took out the card and dialled the number.

A calm voice answered straight away.

'Gerry here, can I help you?'

'Hi, it's Harry. We met yesterday in the café. Could I come and see you please? I've had a really strong dream, which I want to tell you about.'

Gerry gave him his address. Yes, he could see him right away if he cared to come up.

Harry cut across town again. Gerry lived some way up in the old part of town and the steep hill made him slightly breathless as he walked quickly. He must get himself fit again!

Gerry's cottage was small and painted white. Just the number was on the front door, no brass plaque, no clinical smell, or receptionist! The front garden had a few late roses rambling on a trellis, and it was quiet. A robin sat on the fence and trilled a welcome to Harry as he waited.

Gerry flung the door open with a welcoming gesture to enter. It was fairly dark inside. Harry stepped straight into the lounge. A small fire was burning in the grate. The room was simply furnished and a candle was on the table. A grey cat was curled up in the biggest arm chair.

'Good to see you, take a seat!' said Gerry simply.

Harry sat down on the carved wooden chair near the fire as indicated, and Gerry sat down opposite him. He looked at him keenly, especially around his left shoulder as he had done yesterday.

'Eric is ready to say goodbye and move on,' he stated simply. 'Please sit quietly and close your eyes. Just relax and breathe gently.'

No questions, no history taken, no physical examination. Gerry didn't even have any notes in front of him. Harry closed his eyes. He felt quite safe, and calm also.

Gerry came over to his chair and gently rested his hands on his shoulders. He stood for a while like this then moved his hands up to Harry's head. His hands felt warm and comforting. It was like liquid warmth flowing all down Harry's back to his feet. Little tingles of Energy were everywhere.

Gerry moved his hands around him; first one side then another. No pressure, no pain, just a pleasant warm tingling. Harry couldn't remember when he had felt more relaxed or at peace. It was rather like the time he had tried a joint at a party, he thought. But there was no smell of weed in the room, just a faint tinge of incense.

Suddenly there was Eric before him. He looked younger and very happy. He was walking away just like he had in the dream, and he turned and waved his hand.

Harry heard him say quite clearly; "See yer, mate!" then he vanished completely.

The session was over. Gerry gently squeezed his shoulders and stepped back. Harry opened his eyes and was back in the small cosy room. The cat stirred and came over to rub itself against his leg. He felt wonderfully calm and relaxed.

'Eric is now gone,' said Gerry simply. 'When someone dies in a sudden traumatic way they sometimes do not understand what has happened and their Energy remains attached to another person or place. Eric had been so close to you, as a blood brother, that he needed to hang on, until he understood he was really dead. Now he knows and can be released to travel on to better places. He may come back to visit from time to time, but won't disturb or frighten you again. I have also helped you to release some of the negative Energy that enveloped you out in Afghanistan; the fear and hatred that has darkened that whole area. I will need to see you a couple of times more as it goes deep and the body doesn't always want to release it that quickly, but I can see that you will heal well.'

Harry got up smiling. He hadn't felt as good as this in years. He took a note from his wallet and dropped it into the dish on the table.

'Thank you so much!' he said. 'Can I come the same time next week?'

'Sure, I shall look forward to it,' said Gerry embracing him warmly.

Harry felt light as he walked down the hill towards town. What was it that Gerry had meant about Eric being attached to him? It sounded spooky, but in his experience of the last months, also totally logical. All the visions he had had were of Eric in fear and trauma. Now he was free again. It was wonderful. He felt a little sad at the loss of his friend, but so glad that he was now at peace.

Next he must try to get things right with Annie. If he was going to have some more healing sessions he thought it was better to keep that quiet from everyone, as people might think he was really weird. If he could get to a point where he knew what he needed to do next, that would be a good point to relink with Annie. Some time out from the relationship was probably the best thing right now. They both needed some time to relax and heal after their long year of trauma.

He started whistling as he headed through town. He hadn't done that for months either! The crowds were beginning to ooze around the shops and he watched them with interest; before he just wanted to get away from them. Now the whole world looked brighter somehow.

Chapter 16

Harry sat on his sofa bed with the blank page in front of him, chewing the biro. He knew he must be careful how he worded this letter to Annie, so as not to upset her any more, and he really wanted to ensure that their relationship was not over. He was missing her dreadfully, but didn't want to sound needy either.

Dear Annie,
My love for you has not changed! I think about you all the time and wish I could hold you in my arms. I am really sorry I let you down like that and I assure you that there was nothing going on between me and Amanda. I was simply having a bad time with Eric that day.
Things are going well for me here at Molly's and I would really like to see Charlie soon. Could he come here next weekend perhaps? I'll pick him up from school on Friday and drop him back Monday morning if that's ok?
If you've got a flat I assume you want to be independent for a while. I would love to meet and chat about things soon...

He stopped writing and chewed his pen again, not knowing how much pressure to put on her at this point. Maybe just leave it open for now?

Please ring me to confirm this weekend. Thanks a bunch. Love, hugs, Harry XX

He reread the letter several times, wondering how she would receive it. He hadn't given anything away either. They were playing cat and mouse.

He sealed it in an envelope and walked round to Stella and Ted's house and dropped it through the letterbox. Hopefully she would get it soon so that he could see his son at least. He hadn't asked Molly if she would mind if Charlie came round, but he was sure she would enjoy some young company. Charlie hadn't met her very often, but he was a good lad.

Later that evening his phone rang. It was Annie. She had already got the letter, as she had dropped round to her parents' house after school. She sounded relieved but still rather formal. She had been worrying a lot about Harry, especially as Charlie had been asking where he was and when he could see him.

'Yes, that will be ok,' she said. 'I'll let Miss Aitkin know that you'll pick him up, and he can bring his play clothes with him. Don't let him go to bed too late,' she added as an afterthought and then wished she hadn't said it! She rang off without any further comment. He so wished she had chatted a bit. Even the sound of her voice was tantalizing.

He could picture her with her thick brown hair and long lashes framing her big grey/blue eyes. She might be curled up on the sofa with a book or watching TV. He could have put his arms around her and stoked her hair.

In her flat Annie was also agonising. She really wanted Charlie to see Harry, and had willingly arranged the weekend for him, but that meant she would be alone from Friday morning, her day off, until Monday when Charlie got back. 4 days to fill with what? She enjoyed her new flat and her independence and had got in touch with a few old friends as well, but she was missing Harry so much it felt like she was living in a vacuum. Every time her phone rang she hoped it was him. She had been surprised to get the letter, but relieved as it confirmed her own feelings about him. How long were they going to be idiotic like this? Who was going to stop feeling hurt and angry first?

She rang Amanda and asked if she and the girls would like to go to the zoo in Paignton on Saturday. Amanda was thrilled. She found weekends really hard too, and knew that Annie wasn't likely to visit her at the Barracks. Time had dragged since Annie had left.

On Friday Charlie was really excited and kept looking out of the classroom window as the afternoon drew to a close. He loved school and was usually focussed and alert. Today had been different. He had got his sums wrong and had chatted to his friend when they were supposed to be quiet. Miss Aitken knew the reason but couldn't let her brightest pupil get away with bad behaviour. As the bell rang at 3.15 Charlie jumped up and grabbed his bag and coat.

'Can I go out now, Miss? Dad will be here in a minute.' Miss Aitken smiled and let him out into the playground. She watched as Charlie and Harry rushed into each other's arms, and Harry swung him high in the air. She hadn't seen him recently but she thought Harry was looking better than she had seen him for ages. He looked less strained and was grinning from ear to ear.

Harry and Charlie went hand in hand down the road. The sky was clear, although it was chilly. There would be a frost later.

What was there to do with a 7 year old on a dark cold evening in Exmouth? Molly would not want him there all weekend, so Harry had to plan quickly. They would go round to the docks and look at the boats, then maybe walk over to the leisure centre for some supper. He always liked that. There wasn't anything on at the cinema suitable for kids, and anyway Annie didn't approve of him seeing too many films.

They were slightly shy of each other too, as it had been two weeks since they had been together and Charlie didn't know how his Dad would be. Where would he be sleeping tonight?

Walking along looking at the boats broke the ice and they were soon deep in discussion about the kind of boat they would like and the merits of the different shapes. They decided they both liked a small sailing dingy which was moored at the end, with a blue stripe around her.

'Maybe one day we could learn to sail on the river together and get our own boat,' said Harry.

'Dad, are you going away again?' asked Charlie a little anxiously.

'No lad. I'm home for good now. I'm not a soldier any more. We are going to make a new life together one day. Not just yet as Mum and I need to sort out a few things first, but soon we'll all be together again and we can have fun and do things like sailing, eh?'

Although this sounded all rather vague to Harry, it satisfied the young boy, and he skipped happily along beside his Dad until they came to the swimming pool complex. They watched the children having their swimming lessons for a while, and then went to the café for some ham and eggs, with bread and butter, washed down with a glass of milk.

'Tonight you will be staying with Eric's Mum, Molly. She will be pleased to see you again, but you'll have to sleep with me in the lounge,' explained Harry. Charlie thought that would be fun.

'Dad, why did Eric have to die?' asked Charlie suddenly, looking at him very wisely. Harry couldn't answer straight away. Before Gerry's session, a question like this might have sent him into a panic, but now he tried to give a sensible answer to his son.

'He was trying to help save lots of people from getting wounded by the horrid things that blow people up, called IEDs. The Taliban put them in the ground all over the place and sometimes even children would step on them and get really hurt. Eric was very brave to do that, but sadly one exploded the wrong way and killed him. It was very frightening and sad and that's why I've been so upset for so long. Eric has gone to heaven now though and I'm getting better. I won't be scared any more I promise.' Harry said this with such conviction that Charlie breathed deeply in relief and squeezed his Dad's hand across the table.

'Molly must be very sad too,' Charlie commented.

A few minutes later he gazed at Harry with large innocent eyes.

'I'm not going to kill anyone when I grow up! I think it's wrong.'

Coming simply from a child with such directness Harry was shocked but also pleased that his young son could think about things so deeply. He nodded slowly in agreement. Would he ever be able to tell him how he had killed not one but several men, and how pleased he had felt whilst doing it? A sense of shame began to creep through him, in the face of his young idealistic son. Perhaps he could tell him about it when he was older, but not yet.

'Let's go and meet Molly then, shall we,' he suggested, diverting his gloomy thoughts.

They walked back through the dark town hand in hand. The Christmas lights were up already and the town looked quite sparkly and magic. Charlie wasn't often allowed out this late so it was a treat, and he looked around with big eyes.

'Where will we be when Father Christmas comes?' he asked innocently. A pang of pain went through Harry. It wouldn't be a normal Christmas that was for sure. Maybe they could share Charlie between them, so they both got some of the magic of a children's Christmas? Harry pushed the thought aside. It was only November yet, plenty of time to worry about things like that!

Molly was thrilled to see such a grown up boy, looking so like Harry had as a child. He had his colouring and eyes for sure! Maybe a bit of his Mum's character though?

She bustled about making sure that Charlie had everything he needed. He was to sleep on some cushions near Harry's sofa. It was a bit like camping out; quite exciting!

Next morning over breakfast Charlie said,

'Molly do you miss Eric very much?'

Coming straight out with it as he had, with his childlike directness, Molly was caught unawares. Her eyes filled with tears.

'Yes, I do,' she admitted, 'but it's getting a bit better gradually.'

Charlie looked at her intently. He said quietly,

'When you're sad, think of something nice you used to do with Eric and it will make you feel better!'

Coming out with such wisdom from a young child, she was amazed and winked over at Harry, who touselled Charlie's hair and agreed.

'I think we'll take a bus ride today,' Harry suggested. 'Who wants to come to Sidmouth?'

Charlie cheered. He loved bus rides. As it was one of Molly's favourite spots for a day out, she hoped she was included in the suggestion.

'Do you mind if I join you,' she faltered.

'Oh, yes do come too,' said Charlie delighted.

So they all packed up their things and wandered down to the bus station. It was a pretty bus ride and they sat up near the back of the single decker bus, where they had a good view of the countryside. It was still chilly outside, but some of the last of the autumn colours hung to the trees, and the hills showed touches of frost.

They went through the pretty village of Otterton on the way, and Charlie remarked on the thatched cottages. He said he would like to live in one like that, it looked so cosy. Harry had asked him casually about the new flat where he and Annie were. No garden, no bedroom for Annie either. It didn't sound ideal.

Up over a steep hill, the bus grinding along, and then they saw the sea again, lovely and blue in the distance. They dropped down into the town of Sidmouth and got off near the sea and the shops.

There were lots of small gift shops and a huge toy shop where Charlie enjoyed himself for a while.

They had their lunch in a café looking out over the promenade, where lots of old ladies and gentlemen were wandering along with their dogs. It was peaceful here; different from Exmouth.

Time passed so quickly and they all were having a really lovely time. The sun on the beach was warm; Charlie and Harry threw pebbles into the little waves, seeing who could throw furthest, while Molly relaxed on the beach with a magazine she had bought.

At last it was time to catch the bus back. They were amazed how the sun was already sinking behind the hills, with little pink bits of cloud like sheep in a big field.

'I think Eric is up there!' said Charlie unexpectedly, looking up at the changing sunset colours.

'Maybe you're right!' agreed Harry, with a smile. It had been a perfect day spent with his loving son, and he felt really well and happy.

Their weekend together raced by and on Monday morning Harry took Charlie into school. He hugged him goodbye and told him he would see him again soon.

'Why can't you and Mum stop quarrelling, then we could all be together again,' said Charlie suddenly, pouting out his bottom lip as he used to as a little boy when he wanted something. Harry was floored again by his son. What could he say to the child?

'We'll try!' was all he managed, rather lamely.

Chapter 17

Annie was worried about money. She had managed to increase her working hours in Exeter to twenty five a week but she still hadn't enough earnings to meet all the bills and the rent. Her car needed its MOT and Charlie was rapidly growing out of his school shoes. It was stressful living alone with a child. Most evenings she just sat at home and watched telly and they rarely did anything very exciting.

Charlie seemed to be coping alright, so long as he saw Harry regularly. They had arranged, via rather stilted phone conversations, that he would spend alternate weekends at Molly's and also every Wednesday evening. Harry would drop him back to his grandparents before bedtime. That way Annie and he never actually met or saw each other. Annie thought it would be easier that way.

It was now nearly 6 weeks since they had left the barracks. The dark wet weather of December was not helping Annie's mood either. Her Mum had started to worry about her. She was losing weight and she looked anxious and depressed, and was often quite snappy. She had dark rings under her eyes and she looked older.

Her day off was still Friday. On this particular Friday it was cold and wet and she had wandered into the shopping centre to see if she could get a Christmas present for Charlie and also for Amanda's girls. She had found several small things for them, quite cheap, and now she felt tired, so she decided to treat herself to a Cappuccino in her favourite coffee shop on the Strand before going back to the flat. She never liked being in the flat alone. It felt so dreary and empty without Charlie's happy chatter.

'Come on, Annie,' she said to herself as she sipped the warm frothy drink, 'get a grip! You chose this life, didn't you? It's not so bad being a single Mum. At least you have some time for yourself!'

But it didn't feel that way inside. She was lonely and missing Harry. She still didn't know why she didn't make contact. Perhaps it was just hurt pride. He was acting in a very civil way, and was always polite on the phone. Charlie enjoyed having time with him and told her he was much funnier nowadays. What that meant she wasn't sure. Perhaps the split up was doing him good and it was all for the best? He still hadn't got his life together though. He couldn't go on sponging off Molly for ever, could he?

And now Christmas was approaching fast and she hadn't yet fixed up what they were going to do about Charlie. She was dreading it. Time on her own, when everyone else was having a nice family time! Maybe she could go round to her parents, but that wouldn't be a bunch of fun either. Amanda's husband Rod was on leave now, so she didn't really want to bother them as they were having a beautiful 'second honeymoon' together. All her other friends would be having fun together as a family too.

Tears of self-pity welled up. She took out a rather crumpled tissue and blew her nose, trying to hide her face from the other customers in the coffee shop.

A gentle 'ding' sound indicated the door had been opened by another customer coming in. Annie didn't look up straight away as she was still crying. Then she heard a familiar voice say,

'A cappuccino, please!'

She looked up startled. At the counter stood a young man, in jeans and denim jacket, with wavy auburn hair, with his back to her. She looked again not quite sure. He looked so different, and very handsome.

As he turned round he saw her too. Harry came towards her balancing his coffee cup in one hand; he put it down with a thud and came round to her side of the table, and wrapping his strong arms right around her, he kissed her head.

She looked up at him and smiled through her tears.

'What's up lass?' he said gently, looking her up and down.

'It's nearly Christmas,' was all she could think of saying at that moment.

He sat down beside her and took her hand in his. He looked so lovingly at her; she got that warm fluttery feeling in her stomach. Perhaps the whole thing had been one big mistake?

They sat in silence and then started simultaneously to sip their cappuccinos! Then Annie caught Harry's eye and they started to laugh. They had been together so long they understood the slightest innuendo of each other's behaviour and often did the same things at the same time. It was an easy laughter which broke the ice between them, and they felt comfortable in their silence as they finished off their coffees.

'Come on, let's go to your flat where we can have some privacy,' suggested Harry. So Annie gathered up her parcels and they walked hand in hand across the square and down the side streets till they came to the staircase leading up to her flat.

'Good location for everything,' commented Harry, as Annie flung open the front door. Once inside they fell into each other's arms and kissed passionately. What fools they had been, both missing each other like hell.

Once the first kiss was finished, Harry gently undid Annie's coat, then her top and finally her bra. She then undid his shirt buttons and buried her fingers into his hairy chest. She led him through to Charlie's room, which had the double bed in it, and hastily brushed a few toys off the bed, before pulling back the duvet and diving in. Harry was just behind her.

Their love making was gentle and long and they gazed into each other's eyes like two young lovers meeting for the first time. He stroked her thick hair and she nuzzled into his newly grown beard and put her finger tips into his hair, longer now for the first time since before they were married.

Then they lay snuggled up together side by side while they talked and talked. They shared their lonely journeys of the last 6 weeks, their thoughts and feelings and Harry was able to tell her about his experiences with Gerry.

He had been to see Gerry a couple more times and each time he had felt refreshed, stronger and more peaceful. Gerry had encouraged him to write again in the notebook, and he had explored his feelings about his shock, his treatments at the hospital, his loss of self-belief and his anger; putting his innermost feelings onto paper allowed him to release the pain. Part of this too had been about guilt, and his love of Annie and how he might heal the rift between them. He was now so ready and willing to try again, with a less selfish outlook, with more to share.

'Do you think your parents might be willing to give us a Christmas this year?' enquired Harry finally.

'I think they would like nothing better. My Mum hinted at the fact that she was buying a good size turkey this year in case anyone wanted to come round.'

Harry glanced at his watch. It was nearly school pick up time, and the end of term for Charlie. He would have things to bring home from the party they had had today.

'Shall we go down to meet him together and surprise him?' he suggested. Annie nodded. She quickly slipped back into her clothes and brushed her hair before straightening the bed.

'Little does he know what's been going on in his bed!' she laughed.

Chapter 18

Charlie's face when he saw them standing hand in hand at the school gate was a picture! He rushed towards them both and they had a group hug, before Harry lifted him right up on his shoulders as he used to when he was little! Perched up there, Charlie cheered and said,

'Hey, it's going to be a great Christmas! In my letter to Father Christmas which I wrote at school last week, I asked him to make you stop quarrelling! It worked!'

Annie and Harry just squeezed each other's hands. Maybe the Spirit of Christmas was working extra hard for them this year.

They decided to go straight round to Stella and Ted's and forewarn them that they would like to spend a family Christmas together there. As they walked up the garden path together, Stella glanced out of the window and gave an exclamation of pleasure. She opened the door wide to greet them all.

'Look Gran, what Father Christmas did. I asked him in my letter,' said Charlie, looking from one to another.

Stella smiled and just then Ted came in from shutting up the chucks.

'What have we here; a United Front?' he laughed.

'Please can we come for Christmas?' asked Charlie with big eyes. Put like that how could anyone refuse? So it was agreed that they would all spend Christmas Day together, and Charlie could have a sleepover on Christmas night. They didn't forget Molly either, and decided to ask if they could go there for Boxing Day. She was visiting her daughter in Axeminster on Christmas Day itself.

Annie and Charlie walked round to Molly's after they had all had a mug of tea beside Stella's cosy fire. Molly was just preparing supper for Harry, Charlie and herself, as it was Friday night. As they came in, she popped her head out of the kitchen and saw Annie standing shyly there. She went forward and embraced her warmly, realising instantly what was happening.

'We can stretch supper a bit, if you want to stay,' she offered.

'Oh, do have supper with us, Mum,' begged Charlie, not wanting his parents to go their separate ways again.

So they all squeezed around the kitchen table and chatted till way after Charlie's bedtime. At last reluctantly he disappeared off into the lounge, curling up onto the cushions by the sofa, and the adults were left together sharing happy memories of Eric and their teenage days. Molly had always had an open house for the youngsters and Annie and Harry had often included Eric in their adventures. Eric was close now and it felt warm and comfortable in the kitchen.

Annie was walked home by Harry that night, like a proper date, and at the door of her flat he kissed her tenderly again.

'What a couple of sillies we have been, but at least we have learned a lot about appreciating each other. I couldn't have healed myself back at the barracks and it was time for us both to leave. What do you think the coming months will bring for us, now we are setting out on a new life together again?'

'Well I know one thing for sure, and that is that I'm going to see the estate agent in the morning and see if we can get around this 6 month lease somehow. I know the landlord usually does weekly lets for summer visitors, so maybe he'll be ok about my breaking the contract? It would be a bit tight with the three of us here. Do you think he'll be flexible?'

'If we're meant to be together, something will work out,' said Harry pragmatically. He had wondered too though how he could stay on Molly's sofa until May, or share Annie's sofa at her flat. They would need to start looking for their next home quite soon. But first things first! It was Christmas in just 3 days and he hadn't done any shopping yet. He knew what Charlie and he would be doing tomorrow in Exeter; searching out something very special for his dear wife!

When he got back to Molly's, the light was still on in the kitchen; she hadn't gone up to bed as usual. As Harry came in, she called to him quietly. He went to join her.

'Harry, I've been thinking! You, Annie and Charlie need a break in the sunshine together. I don't know when you last had a holiday and you all need a bit of a treat. When Eric was alive I decided to save £10 a week from my pension and give it to him for a deposit on a house when he came out of the army. Of course I never did that, but I've kept the money for a rainy day. I think that rainy day has come! I'd like you to spend the money on a holiday in the New Year, if you can find a good bargain.'

With that she handed Harry a fat brown envelope. He gasped but took it. Inside there were dozens and dozens of £10 notes.

'I think it's about £2000 by now,' she said. 'Have a look on the internet and see if you can get something half decent for that.'

Harry was speechless. He felt so happy, yet also embarrassed to be accepting such a generous gift. It was Christmas though, so he grinned broadly and thanked her warmly. He would start looking on his laptop first thing tomorrow. A holiday was exactly what they all needed, to refresh, bond and take stock of their new lives together.

He lay awake on the sofa for a long time, listening to the gentle breathing of his son beside him, wondering what he should spend the rest of his life doing? He knew it would need be gentle and healing, both for himself and the earth. His experiences out in the war zone had scarred him for life, but he would be able to contribute something useful to society and continue his healing.

Whatever he chose to do must also be right for his wife and son, and maybe another member of the family too? Perhaps they could somehow afford another child, a sister or brother for Charlie? He must ask Annie what she reckoned!

With these happy thoughts he finally drifted into a peaceful sleep.

Chapter 19

Both Harry and Annie woke up next morning with a new sense of purpose and their first waking thought was for each other. Annie hurriedly showered and went out into the cold grey morning towards the estate agent. She explained her dilemma to the blond woman at the desk who had dealt with her before, and she nodded and went into the back office to ring Annie's landlord. It seemed an age until she returned, but she had a big smile on her face.

'Because you are ex-Marines he's going to make an exception for you. He'll charge you the cheap weekly winter rate up until the end of next week, and then forget about the rest. He wishes you well too, by the way. He used to be something important in the forces, I think.'

Annie made a quick calculation. The deposit would more than cover the extra bit she would have to pay doing it this way and she already had paid up a month in advance also, so this deal was affordable. Much relieved she thanked the young lady for her help and rushed outside to ring Harry with the good news.

'Hi, darling, how's your morning going?' he answered cheerily. She explained about the lease and how she would be free to find somewhere new by the end of the next week.

'That's pushing us a bit isn't it? How about going to Tenerife for a fortnight while we hunt for somewhere?'

He was joking of course, thought Annie! But the truth was Harry had been searching online and there was a real bargain to be had, going from Exeter with Thompson's to Los Gigantes to a good hotel, with children coming for free! It was too good to be true. He had counted up the money in the envelope and it was £2300, so they would have enough for a flat deposit too if they needed it, as this holiday was only just over £1000. Amazing!

'No joke!' said Harry. 'I've just booked it! You had better get onto your boss and see if you can get the leave. Shall we ask Molly if she wants to come too; she has been so incredibly generous to us?' Harry explained about her savings in the brown envelope.

'Wow!' was all Annie could say, and after a pause, 'Yes that would be super if she came too. Perhaps she could babysit for us occasionally?'

'You always try to get the best out of every scenario, don't you?' he joked.

'When are we going then?' said Annie.

'The last day of December, leaving at 7a.m. With luck we'll be able to see the New Year in, in the hotel bar! I'll ring them up and make sure we can add another person to the booking. We've already got a 2 bed flat booked, looking over the sea with a balcony! But there is a sofa bed too, in the lounge, I think.'

Annie felt tingly all over with excitement. Had he told Charlie yet, she wanted to know. No, Charlie was with Molly right now, making some scones for tea. Perhaps they should wait till after the Christmas excitement before they told him? But seriously, they would have to have something in the pipeline for when they got back! They couldn't go on depending on everyone's good will indefinitely. Annie would have a look around town and buy the local paper too, as sometimes there were private advertisements.

The phone call over, she headed up Rowle Street where most of the estate agents were, scanning the windows of each one as she went. This was not going to be an ordinary flat, but their new home. It had to be affordable and have some garden too. Everything was really expensive. Harry hadn't yet talked about getting a new job. He was still quite vulnerable to stress and shouldn't push himself too quickly into anything, she knew. But just living on her wage of twenty five hours a week was pushing things too much. They could get some family tax credits perhaps, but she had heard that it was getting harder to apply and she had never asked for any help before. Being in the barracks you were so protected from all these things.

A small frown descended onto her brow. It made her look older and more pinched.

Just then a voice said behind her,

'That's Mrs Kenny isn't it; Annie?' She turned around at the mention of her name. A tall thickset man stood by the pavement looking across at her. He had short hair as did all the Marines, and a slight air of importance. Who was he? She tried to remember the face, putting the khaki uniform on him in her imagination. Then she got it!

'Sergeant Rob Miles?'

He stepped forward and shook her hand warmly.

'I'm so glad to see you, I have been wondering how your poor husband has been faring since I last saw him. It has been a hard time for him, hasn't it?'

She nodded. How much did he know, and was he aware that Harry had left Lympstone now? In order not to seem rude, she suggested that they go into Sue's Pantry just across the road for a coffee. She told him that Harry was in Exeter today with Charlie, now 7 years old.

As they sipped their coffee, she began carefully to fill him in on some of the details of their life in the last year or so, leaving out the bits that were embarrassing, like splitting up and the muddle with Amanda. She assured Rob that Harry was much better now and looking for his next step.

'Is that why you were scanning the estate agents windows?' he asked.

She explained that they were looking for a long-term let, a proper home where Harry could work in the garden and continue his healing.

Rob looked thoughtful for a moment.

'You know I have an idea! The Clinton Devon Estates have several properties locally which they rent out long-term. I know the Estates Manager quite well and he was mentioning a place which was coming up in a few weeks' time, near Otterton. There are various clauses attached to going in there. Like doing some maintenance work; but I think it might just suit you. It is usually taken by word of mouth, by locals who know the landlord, if you get me! I'll make some enquiries for you and get back to you, if you could let me have your number to ring.'

This seemed like a dream come true. Annie hurriedly scribbled down her number on a paper napkin and handed it to Rob. She couldn't wait to hear more about it. She knew that Rob would have the connections to get it for them, if it were suitable.

'Do give my regards to Harry, and it's been so nice seeing you again,' said Rob affably.

Annie and he left the coffee shop and headed off in opposite directions. Annie felt she needed to pray now. She hadn't ever been religious but at this moment she made her way across to the church as if by instinct. She crept into the quiet echoing space and sat down in a pew looking around her. She didn't even know any prayers. But her heart was saying it all. Please, please, please let there be a home where she, Harry and Charlie could make a new start together and be happy and healthy! That was all she asked. She sat there with her eyes closed thinking this as hard as she could, then left the church by the back door and made her way home in the dusky afternoon light.

The rest of the evening was spent wrapping presents, with the TV on as company. At about 9.30 she was going to head for bed, when her phone rang. She jumped and grabbed it. Perhaps it was Harry needing a chat? It was the resonant voice of the Sergeant.

'Well Annie, if I may call you that, I had a chat with my friend the Estates Manager and he is willing that you have a look at that place I mentioned to you this afternoon. I gave you a glowing reference of course,' he added with a chuckle. 'Could you make it over there tomorrow afternoon, as they are quite keen to get the lease tied up this side of Christmas, as Mr Arkwright is off to the Canaries afterwards?'

It was Sunday tomorrow, the day before Christmas Eve! She agreed they would meet him and Mr Arkwright at 3p.m, and he gave her instructions as to how to get there. She just hoped that Harry and Charlie were free to come then. It was all falling into place, but so fast she could hardly keep up!

She rang Harry and told him the good news. He was sounding quite tired after a long afternoon in Exeter with Charlie. The Christmas shopping rush had been rather much for his nerves. He still needed quiet and rest, she thought. A place in the country would be ideal for them, and still near enough to Exmouth and Charlie's school, and commutable to Exeter for work.

'Don't get your hopes up too high,' Harry warned, sounding a bit depressed, 'these places are like gold dust. They will pick the person with the best references.'

Chapter 20

Next afternoon, dressed in there tidiest country clothes, they all stood outside a dear little cottage, on a quiet lane near Otterton. It all felt like a dream. There was a thatched roof and roses around the door, just like the ones that Charlie had liked. Behind the cottage there was a big garden, rather overgrown now as the last tenant had become elderly and unable to keep it up, but definite signs of a vegetable patch and a hen run in the back corner; there were some apple trees too and a pond where once some fish had been. An old black cat was washing itself near the front door and a winter robin was singing its heart out on a bush covered with holly.

Next door to the cottage was a working farm, with a neat yard where the cows came in to be milked twice a day, a tractor and some other bits and pieces of farm machinery. Perhaps Harry might pick up some work there?

Just then a car roared around the corner with two men in it. It seemed too shiny and posh for a country lane. It slewed to a halt and out got Rob and another man with grey hair and a rather military moustache.

Rob and Harry briefly embraced in a slightly embarrassed way, and Mr Arkwright shook all their hands.

'So you and Rob knew each other out in Afghanistan in action, I hear?' said Mr Arkwright. 'Rather you than me, I'd say! I was around for the Falklands but didn't get involved much, as I was mainly on the ground by then.'

He looked Harry up and down critically, as though he were buying a new filly. Annie didn't take to him, but said nothing. Charlie piped up,

'Can we live in this house, please? It's just the kind I was dreaming about!'

Rob grinned from ear to ear, and Mr Arkwright said, 'Well, let's just go inside, shall we, and see if your parents approve too!'

He led them into the front room of the cottage. There were old oak beams, and an open fireplace with a basket of logs stacked up ready. The place felt a little neglected, but Annie was already seeing things she could do to cheer it up; new curtains, a rug in front of the fire, and a couple of new pictures. It wasn't furnished, and their furniture would fit in well with the age of the property. Most of it had come from auction rooms anyway, so they could always gradually replace it.

Behind the lounge was a galley kitchen, with a rather tatty electric cooker, and an old china sink, which nowadays was quite trendy. Then out at the back was a space for the washing machine, wellies and coats. The back door was shabby too, but could easily be renovated with some new paint, and it led out into a back yard where there was a washing line and then the garden. That was the best bit. The afternoon winter sun showed up its potential. It was good earth and well sheltered from winds too, with a hedge all around it, ideal for growing their food. The hen run was sound and the fruit trees would be fine once they were pruned a bit. The quiet was wonderful. Harry stood and breathed deep. Yes, this was the place where he wanted to be!

They went upstairs then and Charlie rushed into the little front room which looked out over the farm next door.

'This can be my room, so I can see the cows coming in!' he announced.

The back room was away from the lane, so even quieter, and would get the morning sun slanting into it. The window sill was wide and Annie could imagine herself sitting there reading, on a new long cushion made to fit, looking out over the garden; bliss!

A door with a latch was at the bottom of the stairs to keep the draughts out on winter evenings. The heating system was antiquated but Mr Arkwright informed them he was getting a plumber to put in oil fired central heating. It should be ready by about mid-January, he thought. That would mean a certain amount of touch up decorating too, but he was sure they would be up to that?

Because of the basic condition of the cottage and the work involved, Mr Arkwright had set the rent low, not much more than a council dwelling. They would be able to afford it, if Harry found some part-time work too.

Harry and Annie could hardly breathe, they so much wanted him to say that they had first offer of refusal. At last he said it, and they immediately both agreed they would like to have a long lease on it, without even discussing it together. It was there's! Now they could have Christmas and their holiday together in the sound knowledge that they had a home to come back to, albeit a modest one.

As Rob and Mr Arkwright started up the lane with a roar of the powerful engine, Annie, Charlie and Harry opened the latch gate once more and walked round into the back garden. They stood quietly listening to the sounds of nature, the goodnight song of the thrush and blackbird and the gentle whispering of the wind in the bushes. They peered over the hedge to see what was beyond, and they came face to face with a shaggy pony, inquisitive as to who was there.

'Maybe I could learn to ride too', said Charlie wistfully.

On the way back down the high street with its thatched cottages, they noticed a sign to the village school. They turned off the road and saw a small school building nestled up near the church. The notice board outside gave them an inkling that it was very parent active, and run well.

'How would you like to walk to school here?' Harry asked Charlie.

'That would be really cool,' he said.

They would make contact with the headmistress after Christmas and see if they had space for Charlie locally, rather than driving everyday into Exmouth. It made much more sense, rather than having to buy another car.

It was getting dusky and they all felt hungry after an early lunch, so they wandered into the village pub, which did good bar meals and treated themselves to pie and chips, sitting at the table near a roaring log fire.

Christmas decorations were up and the tree twinkled with its many lights. They were so happy together it was almost as though Christmas had already started for them. Tomorrow night Father Christmas would come to them, but they felt He had already dropped by early and brought them a big present of a new home to share together.

Chapter 21

Christmas Eve as always was a very busy time for all of them. Stella was baking and cooking, making sure that there was enough food in the house; she was starting to panic that she hadn't bought enough.

Ted was relegated to putting up the little plastic tree with its baubles and lights. That was always his job. He enjoyed the quiet relaxation of it, while everything around him was spinning!

Harry was trying to decide what to get for his in-laws and Molly. He always left his present buying till the last minute and now was trailing around Exmouth, realising he couldn't spend as much as he would like to, but trying to find a little something for each one of them which was appropriate.

Finally he got back to Molly's feeling strung out. She made him a mug of tea, and he disappeared into the lounge to wrap everything up.

Molly was preparing a huge trifle for Boxing Day. She knew she wouldn't have time tomorrow, as she was off early to Axeminster. She went to her daughter's house every Christmas day. It was not that easy now that Eric was no longer with them. Her only daughter was rather like her ex-husband, neurotic and tight. She worked in a bank and had an immaculate flat which she was very proud of. They always had a ready prepared frozen turkey breast, which tasted like cardboard and salt, and then a tiny Christmas pudding from Tesco, draped in brandy butter; then the Queen at 3p.m after they had washed up the two plates. It was rather grim really.

She was very much looking forward to having the family round on Boxing Day when things would be fun. They might play some board games, have crackers and she would give them cold ham and salad, which they could eat whenever they liked. She scooped out the custard onto the fruit, jelly and cake, liberally laced with cheap sherry and sighed. How she missed her Eric at such times! He would always come into the kitchen and help her, and want to lick out the bowl after she had whipped the cream.

She felt a warm breath near her neck and was instantly comforted. He was ever near her and was giving her support from the Other Side, of that she was sure.

Annie had to work until lunch time on Christmas Eve. She had asked her boss about the holiday and he had seemed very pleased that things were working out better for the couple. He had offered her a couple of extra days at the end too to get sorted with the new cottage. She was so lucky having a job like this, and she was always a good worker. Now they were preparing the party in the office. There were few calls on a day like this, and one of the girls took it in turns to man the phone.

Finally at noon they clocked off and opened some bubbly. The nibbles were all laid out on plastic plates and they even had some party poppers to make a bit of cheer. They raised their glasses.

'Happy Christmas, everyone! And here's to Annie and her handsome man; and may she have a fab second honey moon!' Everyone laughed and toasted her.

'Thank you, especially for all your support,' was all Annie could say, her eyes filled with tears.

When she finally left the office at about three, she spun back to the flat to wrap her presents, tidy up and then went to fetch Charlie from his friend. Being a single parent she had had to rely heavily on friends to look after Charlie at such times. It wasn't easy working and being a full-time single Mum, even with parents and friends around, and only working part-time hours.

She planned to take him to the crib service this evening, at the church, as she felt she owed a big 'Thank you' to someone; whoever was looking after them. She had never been religious, but realised her prayers had been answered, so maybe just a 'Thank you' was in order now!

Charlie and she walked up to the big parish church. The path leading up to the big porch and open door were full of parents with their children. She recognised a few from the school playground and smiled at them. She was feeling a little shy now in this new environment.

Charlie was keen to get a seat and pulled her into the already crowded church. Candles were lit, and a huge Christmas tree was glistening from top to toe.

'Can we sit near the front, so we can see Baby Jesus in the crib?' he asked. They squeezed their way forward to the front pew where just two seats remained.

The organ boomed and everyone sang the carols which they knew so well. A warm rush of appreciation glowed through Annie. Not only had she got a wonderful son, family and friends, but her husband was loving and caring. They were soon going to spend special time together in the warm sunshine, and then have the excitement of creating a new home in the country. Everything was perfect!

After the service and mince pies and a glass of wine, she walked back to the flat with her son. He yawned loudly as they sat over their supper.

'Early to bed for you, my lad, or Father Christmas won't come!' She teased.

Charlie didn't argue. He was so looking forward to tomorrow, spending time together as a family at his grandparents' house. The sooner he slept, the sooner it would come!

Having put his red felt stocking, which Molly had bought him, at the end of his bed, he snuggled down and was soon asleep. Annie texted Harry to tell him that the coast was now clear, and he was soon tapping gently on her door, bringing a few bits with him for the stocking. They sat side by side on the sofa wrapping presents, being as quiet as they could. The job done, Annie made them a warm drink and they cuddled up together and watched some late TV.

It was nearly midnight, and Harry yawned now too.

'I'd better be pushing off,' he said reluctantly. 'Tomorrow night we can be together in a decent bed, but for now the sofas have to suffice.'

He kissed her tenderly.

'If you see Father Christmas around as you walk back, make sure you thank him from us all,' said Annie.

'Sure thing, darling!' Harry replied, and went down the steps into the dark starlit night.

Next morning Charlie slept until it was light. Many children had been awake for hours, but Annie was just stirring too, so she got into the big double bed with him and watched happily as he unwrapped all his parcels. His face lit up as he found a big packet of sunflower seeds amongst the rest of the bits and pieces.

'Now I can help Dad in our new garden, and plant sunflowers all around the front. That will look great in the summertime,' he enthused.

Later they walked over to Stella and Ted's, and Harry was already there, helping Ted get some yule logs in. The turkey was beginning to smell good and the presents under the tree were piled up ready.

There were big hugs and 'Happy Christmases' all round, and then they got going on the vegetable preparation and opened the sherry bottle. The sun filtered through the lounge window. It would be nice for a walk along the front by the sea after lunch.

After the stupendous turkey meal, which they ate in the sitting room with the log fire blazing, on Ted's trestle table from the garage covered with the best white cloth, they all felt too full to move for a bit, but after a while Harry suggested,

'Let's take the car down to the far end of the beach and walk off some of this, shall we.'

Ted's legs were none too good these days, but he could have a short walk on the flat, so they agreed and were soon wandering along the sea front with half the population of Exmouth! There were dogs of every shape and colour, children with their new bikes, grannies in wheelchairs well wrapped up in blankets against the cold and couples holding hands.

Harry and Annie went a little ahead of the others, arm in arm, gazing at the twinkling waves and the seagulls swooping, hopeful of some Christmas dinner too. Ahead of them they saw a couple holding hands with a little girl on a new scooter and a toddler in a push along toy. Both girls were wearing matching bobble hats and scarfs. Annie suddenly whooped for joy and ran to meet them. It was Amanda and her husband Rod and the girls. They had been so fully occupied that she hadn't got around to ringing her with all the news.

Now Amanda looked at them with shining eyes as she saw that they were back together, and they all hugged each other.

'I've really missed you Annie,' she said. They told her about their holiday and the new house.

'I'll be over with my paint brush and dungarees,' laughed Amanda, and Annie knew her friend would be as good as her promise. The girls were happy to see her too. They all walked along the prom together for a while, until Ted announced he was going back to the car now. So wishing them a delightful second honeymoon and promising to keep in touch, Amanda and Rod left them to their walk. The family returned home to Stella's mighty fruit cake decorated with snowmen and icing sugar children playing on top.

Charlie looked up from his new Lego set which had been keeping him quiet since their return.

'You know, I think this has been my best Christmas ever!'

The others agreed with him.

Much later, with Charlie safely tucked up in bed at Stella's, Harry and Annie walked back to the flat through the quiet town together, tottering a little after a late drink; 'just one for the road' as Ted had said. They looked up at the bright stars and laughed together at nothing in particular.

'We'll be in bed all night together again,' mused Harry. Enforced separation this time was even sweeter than it had been when Harry came back on leave stressed and tired after his time out in Afghanistan.

'And 'till death us do part',' said Annie with a happy little sigh.

They lit some candles in the bedroom when they got back to the flat, and soon dived into bed together, snuggling up to keep warm.

'Yes definitely the best Christmas ever, as Charlie said,' they agreed.

Chapter 22

Those days after Christmas simply flew by. Annie had to work on several days between the bank holidays, and Charlie spent some happy days with Harry, either at Molly's or with Annie's parents. The weather held fine, so they were able to go out for walks and play football together in the park, one of Charlie's favourite occupations at present. His favourite Christmas present had been a new football and his pride and joy. Harry had never enjoyed football much at school, but now he took a renewed interest as he showed his young son the different types of kick and taught him some of the rules of the game.

They had told Charlie on Boxing Day about the pending holiday and he had been thrilled.

'Will I get to go on a big aeroplane?' he asked eagerly. They showed him on Gran's big atlas how far it was, and that it was on the same latitude as northern Africa, so would be nice and warm and sunny most days.

Annie had to find the right clothes for herself and Charlie amongst all the piles of things she had grabbed from the barracks' house at the last minute. She discovered quite a few essentials were missing for a holiday abroad, so she dashed out in her lunch break to see if she could find any bits and pieces in the Exeter sales. She remembered reading somewhere that you could buy cheap summer clothes in Tenerife, so she wasn't too bothered when she discovered everything for sale was winter-weight. They would just buy clothes when they got there!

Harry would have to sort his own stuff out at Molly's. He also found he was missing a few vital things, so he popped out to the shops one afternoon on his own to search out a couple of new t-shirts.

Amongst all the excitement they were clearing up the flat, as they would have to leave the keys at the agents on the morning of the 31st, dropping them through the letterbox on their way to the airport. They could store everything neatly at the back of Ted's garage, ready to move into the cottage when they came back. Annie spent several evenings repacking all Charlie's toys and her bits and pieces which were strewn around the flat. She also managed to contact the removal firm to arrange a move-in date with them. Everything was so difficult between Christmas and New Year as most firms were closed.

Molly was also getting in a panic thinking about her pending holiday. It was years since she had been away anywhere and several more since she had flown in an aeroplane. She had to buy a new suitcase, as her old one was so battered.

Her passport only had a few months left to run on it too, but enough to get her there and back, she hoped. She needed travel insurance too, which Harry sorted out for her one evening on his laptop.

Bits of paper with lists of 'to do's' were everywhere and several times things went missing. It was all good fun though and no-one got stressed out too badly or lost their temper.

The 31st of December dawned grey and a bit warmer. There had been some fog earlier in the week, but all was now clear.

As their flight was so early they took a taxi, picking up first Annie, with all her luggage, and then Charlie, who was spending the last night at Gran's, then Molly and Harry. He had been helping Molly turn off the water, and put the heating system on low. You never knew at this time of year if England would have a sudden freeze.

They checked they had their passports, their printed off boarding passes and all their belongings, seven pieces of luggage in all!

Harry hadn't flown since coming back on the big C17 to Brize Norton last year, after he had spent some time in the psychiatric hospital in Germany. They had sent him there for some reason as the British place wasn't suitable or was full up. Either way, he had been separated from the family for some time and it had been HELL! Annie had come out to see him a couple of times, but their conversations had been strained and he didn't remember a huge amount about it now, because of the effect of the drugs he had been given. All those drugs were nearly out of his system now. He had dumped the rest of them at the pharmacist one morning after he moved in with Molly.

Now he was flying on a Boeing 737 from Exeter airport, so very different, but he was still secretly a bit nervous. He also was feeling stressed because of packing up his temporary home at Molly's. Her warmth and motherly care had made him feel secure and nurtured.

Once they got back he would be the head of the household again and would need to make decisions and keep track of their finances.

He kept these worries to himself, but they had affected his sleep this week and sometimes he would wake up in a sweat, with dark thoughts swirling around his mind. He didn't realise that the rich food and extra drink he had had over Christmas was also affecting him, putting a strain on his liver and altering his mood. Coming off all those drugs wasn't easy either, but he was determined to do it.

He put a brave face on everything though and held Charlie's hand tightly as they queued up to go through the security check. He pointed out the various things of interest to the lad, such as the x-ray machine and the dog who sat patiently nearby ready to sniff out anything suspicious.

Annie was keeping a friendly eye on Molly, as she was a bit flustered too. She was wearing a huge cream sunhat with a blue ribbon, which she had once worn at a wedding. She thought it would come in handy for the sun.

They waited patiently in the departure lounge until their plane was called. Exeter airport was so small and friendly that Harry's fears disappeared again, and he looked forward to sharing his son's first flying experience with him.

He went over to the café and bought everyone a drink and some crisps. Then he took Charlie off to see the duty-free shops while Annie and Molly chatted and people watched. They had become close over the last few weeks of toing and froing and Molly was pleased to have a 'second daughter', so different from her own.

She really liked Stella too and their lifelong connection and friendship had grown even stronger in recent weeks. Stella would check her home for the post, and water the plants while she was gone.

Since Eric's passing they had lost touch somehow. It often happened like that; when a disaster happens people are often embarrassed to make contact, in case they say the wrong thing. Annie and Harry had broken that ice for them and now she knew she had a strong friend in Stella again.

Molly was a bit sad really that Harry, Annie and Charlie were moving out of Exmouth. She would miss the young company. But they had promised faithfully they would keep in touch and had decided to share their Sundays together with her at each other's houses, once they were settled in. Now she had two whole weeks of their company to look forward to.

At last the gate number was announced on the electronic flight board and they gathered up their hand luggage and made their way to the queue which was forming. There seemed to be mainly English people on the plane, older couples and a few families with young children. There were no school aged children now, since the government had clamped down.

Harry had managed to write to Charlie's headmistress, amidst everything else he'd done this last week. He had explained that the family were getting back together again and that it was important that Charlie spent time together with his reunited parents. If that didn't work he was prepared to pay the £60 fine. But yesterday a white envelope had popped through Molly's door with a formal acceptance of his request, which was a relief. He was surprised it had all worked out at such short notice in the Christmas holidays.

He had also written a letter to Otterton Church of England School, enquiring whether Charlie could have a place when they got back. They hadn't heard yet, but Stella would look out for a likely envelope at Molly's, and text them with any news.

They went down the long stuffy corridor and were greeted at the plane door by the hostesses. They smiled kindly at Charlie, who looked at them up with big eyes. He sat by the window and Harry was next, with Annie on the aisle seat. They fastened their seat belts, Harry helping Charlie with his. As the plan started to rev up Harry went hot and cold and his palms started to sweat. Annie glanced at him and took his hand firmly in hers.

'We're off on our second honeymoon,' she whispered in his ear. He had started to shake again, but hearing her voice he took a very deep breath, blew it out again, felt his feet on the ground and focused his mind, as Gerry had taught him to do. The panic attack passed as quickly as it had started and they were off!

Charlie had his face glued to the window, and turned to Harry with shining eyes.

'Dad, how can something this big and heavy just go up in the sky?' he asked with wonder.

Harry managed a laugh at his young son's question.

'It's called aerodynamics' he replied. 'When you're older you'll learn all about it in physics.'

Charlie thought he would like that very much, and gazed back out of the window at the tiny houses below, now disappearing into the mist. Soon he could see nothing at all and then suddenly they were out in bright sunshine, with huge billowing clouds underneath them and a deep blue sky.

Charlie thought he had never seen anything so beautiful, and imagined Father Christmas in his sleigh travelling through clouds like these. He whispered a big 'Thank you' to him again for all the wonderful things which were happening to him.

Molly sat two rows back from the family. She had read and reread the emergency instructions in the pocket in front of her, then got out her new magazine which Harry had bought for her. The lady next to her seemed friendly so she launched into a conversation with her, which ended up with them exchanging addresses and phone numbers by the time they reached Tenerife! She was local to Exmouth too, so she had found a new friend; someone who didn't know about her history and grief. That was a good new venture! They agreed to meet for a coffee on their return.

Annie nodded off, her head on Harry's shoulder. She was beginning to relax after all the stress of the last weeks. She didn't realise how tired she was until just now. She was going to enjoy a relaxing holiday in the sunshine, doing absolutely nothing!

Harry got out some playing cards and he and Charlie spent some time playing 'Snap' in whispers, so as not to wake up Annie. They found it hilarious and laughed together like two naughty boys; then Harry fished out a packet of liquorice toffees and together they managed to nearly finish off the packet, saving just two for Molly and Annie. Harry's boyish fun and sense of humour was going to resurface this holiday. He didn't need to be either a severe father, a stressed out soldier following the rules, or a patient with PTSD! He was going to reinvent himself and enjoy life with his family.

By the time the four hour flight was over and they stepped out onto the hot tarmac in the bright sunshine, it was four very different people who started their holiday together.

Chapter 23

They all decided they loved Tenerife. Their apartment in the hotel was conveniently located for the shops and the beach and they had a glorious view of the mighty cliffs from their balcony. Every morning when they woke up the sun was just peeping over the high hills behind the town, casting shadows on the cliff face. The sea looked very blue and the white apartment blocks, clinging to the hillsides, all with balconies facing the sea view, looked like hundreds of little eyes staring downwards towards the harbour with its busy boats.

Harry and Annie slept on the pull-out sofa, as they were always the last to go to bed. But it was quite comfortable. Charlie had his own room where he could play quietly, and Molly had the best room facing the sea, with its own balcony. She spent many happy hours out there sunning herself on the lounger, reading a book or doing a crossword puzzle. She didn't have a care in the world and had never felt better. All her aches and pains from the damp Devon air disappeared and she felt herself growing younger, as she lost weight and managed to climb up all the steep hills in the town. She got a nice tan too, and bought a few new clothes with her pension money which she had saved up.

'This is the life!' she said to herself, 'I wonder if I would ever get bored of that view? I expect though I would miss my friends eventually.' She did take a sneaky peek at the estate agents windows though as she walked by!

Often in the evenings after they had eaten, and Charlie had gone to bed, she would watch telly while the 'youngsters' as she called them would go into town and find some entertainment at one of the many cafes or hotels. She enjoyed the quiet space of the flat on her own too.

Annie and Harry took these times to really enjoy each other's company in a way they hadn't for years. Sometimes they danced together to a live band or solo singer, or walked hand in hand above the rocky coves on the wide walkways, watching the moon on the water. Sometimes they went to a bar and people watched, or chatted idly about this and that. They often kissed and they found new joy in their physical closeness.

The days just sped by, and soon they were into their second week.

They went on a coach tour of the whole island, and still thought their corner was the prettiest, and they went on local busses to some of the other nearby villages, exploring down the coastline.

They went to Los Christianos and found it too full of bustle and tourists for their liking. Every day was full and satisfying, but with no sense of rush or needing to complete anything definite.

Charlie was a joy to be with. He had tried swimming in the pool but found it rather chilly at this time of year, so was content to play on his own or chat to whoever was willing to listen to his happy prattle, and join in everything that was suggested.

One morning quite early Annie woke up and thought she felt a bit sick. Maybe the prawns she had enjoyed at the restaurant last night? Then a thought occurred to her and her stomach turned over in shock and excitement. Her period was at least two weeks overdue and her breasts felt slightly tingly. She couldn't be, could she? She rechecked her dates and yes, she was definitely well overdue. She hadn't really thought about it before but now she also remembered the afternoon when she and Harry had made love at the flat after their cappuccinos. That was when it had happened!

Harry was still fast asleep. The doves were cooing outside the window and the pink apricot light of dawn was just creeping up the cliffs. She went quietly to the loo so as not to disturb anyone then got back into the bed beside Harry. He stirred.

'Harry' she whispered in is ear. He grunted 'Are you awake?'

'I could be!' he murmured sleepily.

'I've got something to tell you. I think I'm pregnant. How would you like to be a Daddy again?'

Harry sat bolt upright, then hugged her tightly in his arms, nearly squeezing all the air out!

'I should like nothing better; a little sister for Charlie, another of his wishes!'

'How do you know it's not a boy?' demanded Annie.

'I know!' said Harry even surprising himself, 'And her name is Belinda.'

Chapter 24

They decided not to tell anyone about the pregnancy for a while yet, and continued to enjoy their holiday right up to the last minute. It felt very cold in England when they got back, but they had many happy memories of a magical holiday, and a good tan to show off. They all felt much better for their time away.

On their return, Annie went back to work and Charlie started at his new school. It was quite different from his last one, but he loved it and soon had friends from the village knocking at the door, asking him to play.

Their move into the cottage had gone really smoothly and Harry spent most of his time now doing decorating, and improvements, Annie helping too at weekends. Amanda, true to her word had been over to help them too. Harry had even done some gardening and clearance outside when the weather was warm enough, on those early spring days. He had prepared the vegetable beds ready for sowing later and went over to the neighbouring farm to beg some cow manure to help the crops along.

Stan was the farmer and ran his rented farm well for the Clinton Devon Estates. He had a good herd of mixed milking cows and also some bullocks for meat rearing. He had a couple of fields of winter wheat too coming along well in the spring sunshine.

Charlie had gone over one day and watched fascinated as the cows walked into the yard and were hooked up to the milking machines. He saw for himself the white milk coming down the pipe and wondered why green grass turned into white milk! The children at the farm were a bit older than him, but the girl, Sally, was in his school and she let him pet the pony sometimes, until one day he had found the courage to ask if he could have a ride.

She helped him into the saddle and took him around the field a couple of times, while he sat up proudly and pressed his knees into the pony's sides as she instructed him. He loved it, and asked afterwards if he could do it again.

'Sure,' she had answered.

One day when Annie was out at work, there was a knock on the back door. Harry opened it and Stan stood there in his wellies, which were coated with dung from the yard. Harry asked him in and Stan took off his boots before stepping inside, smelling gently of the cow dung on his dungarees.

They hadn't had much of a conversation before, but Harry felt easy with this quiet gentle man; a man of the earth. His wife and children had been more forthcoming and chatted in the lane to Annie when she was coming to and fro.

'I need some help,' began Stan, his big hands in his pockets. 'Fred, that's my cowman, 'as gone off sick with bronchitis. He gets it sometimes at this time o' year. I knew you were 'ome and wondered if you fancied learning 'ow to do them cows?' he spoke with a gentle Devon bur, which was pleasing to the ear.

Harry nodded eagerly. He hadn't been across to ask about work yet as he had been so busy with the cottage, but he knew he should try and get some paid work soon.

Stan continued; 'If you can come across this evening, 'bout five, I'll show you what needs to be done. Going rate is £8 an hour.'

Harry agreed gladly. So that evening after Annie got home and was putting her feet up on the sofa, while Charlie practised his reading with her, Harry put on his large boots and his oldest jeans and went across to the milking shed.

Stan issued him with a huge rubber apron and a special hat which covered all his hair, and showed him where things were kept.

The cows were already all in the yard and the first ladies were filing into the shed looking forward to their cow nuts which came down a chute into a metal trough from above. The soft regular whirr of the milking machines and their munching put them in the right mood for the milk to flow.

Stan showed Harry how to clean off the udders of each cow with a wet cloth and then position the four suction teats over the cow's udders. Almost as soon as they were on, the frothy white liquid began to flow down the tube and along a pipe into the main tank where it was cooled quickly. The tanker would collect it early in the morning, taking it to the dairy, for pasteurising, packaging or making into yoghourt.

Harry went along the row of cows, opening and closing their gates, putting on the teats and washing them. The work was relaxing and rhythmical and the munching cows were happy with their new cowman.

After an hour or so, Harry saw that the front yard was empty, the cows now waiting patiently to return to the field. He went with Stan up the lane with the cows, their udders now empty and comfortable. He whooped at them to get a move on, and the lovely collie dog ran at the back ensuring there were no stragglers.

They came to their field and Stan went on ahead to open the gate, leaving Harry in charge of the cows. It felt good and safe to be guiding a group of gentle beasts along a Devon lane. He looked around him and smiled. If this was what being a cowman entailed, he was up for it!

He tramped back down to the farm with Stan in his big boots.

'I'm happy, if you are' said Stan in a friendly manner. Harry nodded.

And so it was that from then on Harry milked the cows, morning and evening. He liked getting up very early and creeping downstairs before the others were up. The dawn was a good time to be alive.

The other cowman never came back, because his chest was too bad, so Harry continued the work quite happily. Sometimes there were other jobs that Stan needed help with too; hedging along the lanes, harvesting the wheat and mending fences. As Harry was strong and active he could put his hand to most things, and he was quiet and pleasant too, 'reliable' as Stan remarked to a friend.

The pay wasn't great, but Annie had overcome her qualms and applied for Family Credit for them, so if they were careful they could manage their day to day costs alright. Both of them felt it was better to be happy than rich.

As summer approached Annie's swelling belly made them all feel really excited. Charlie had been thrilled to hear he was going to get his little sister at last. The scan had confirmed it was a girl, though Harry knew all along somehow. Annie was busy creating a snug crib for her, with a little hood to keep off the draughts. Molly and Stella were both knitting busily and Amanda had found loads of the girls' off casts up in the attic for Annie to sort out.

'There's no point in spending loads on clothes when they aren't aware what they look like,' she advised pragmatically, 'There'll be enough time for the fashion parade later on, once they start school.'

Annie's job ended in late July, when she was going on maternity leave. She wanted to return to work, after she had stopped breast feeding and felt this was possible, given Harry's situation. He would be at home when she was at work, and any gaps would be gladly filled by Molly or Stella.

Harry was really looking forward to being a proactive Dad and a housefather. His cooking skills were coming on to, although he had always enjoyed being in the kitchen.

His days were full and busy. The garden was beginning to really look good now with a sprouting vegetable patch, hens scratching in their run in the corner and the fruit trees looking healthy and productive. He had made contact with the beekeepers association too and had been promised some help to find a second hand hive and a summer swarm.

One early June day when it was hot and sultry and he was just picking some salads for supper, a man drew up outside the gate and called to him.

'Are you the chap who wants some bees?' Harry nodded.

'You got a free moment?' the man said. Harry locked up the cottage and got into the chap's van and they drove quickly to the other side of the village. The man introduced himself as Bill. Harry had seen him once at the beekeepers meeting. He had two bee suits in the back of his van, and a serviceable but slightly battered hive and some boxes and frames filled with wax.

'I can let you have this lot for £30.' Bill said. Harry realised it was an absolute bargain, but was enough to get him started on his new venture, so he paid Bill straight away. Once they found the swarm it was busy and engrossing. The bees had settled in the top branches of an old apple tree and Bill borrowed a ladder to reach them. Harry watched as he knocked the big swarm down into the box he had brought. He didn't wear his bee suit or gloves, which Harry thought very odd.

'They won't sting you while they're busy swarming. They are concentrating on staying together with their Queen. Once they settle in the new hive they may be a bit tetchier,' said Bill. 'You've got a good swarm here though to get you started. They look healthy too.'

Once back at the cottage Bill took the hive and the frames and positioned them in the far corner of their garden, facing southeast and with a clear flight path in front of the hive. He stood the hives on some bricks and made sure it was stable.

'You got a scythe or shears?' said Bill. Harry rummaged in the old shed, which had been left full of useful bits and pieces and produced some slightly rusty but still workable shears. He watched Bill as he expertly clipped away at the long grass in front of the hive.

'There you are; a palace for them! You'll need to keep this grass short though.' Bill advised. He then went to the van and produced the box of bees and set it down near the entrance. The trusting little creatures flew around for a few moments, and then filed into the new hive like so many soldiers, Harry thought. The Queen was there amongst them, leading her troops, just like the Sergeant had done. Watching these wonderful creatures and learning to treat them with gentle respect but firmness would be the final healing step for Harry.

Their wonderful sweet harvest of honey was a bonus which human beings have learnt to value over many thousands of years and endlessly search for. It is the Sweetness of Life.

Harry felt content as he watched in awe as they moved in and out of the hive, cleaning and preparing it for their new babies, just as he was doing to the cottage for Belinda, he thought amused. He was like the housekeeper bees!

Later that day, with Charlie and Annie home again, they decided to eat their tea in the garden. Harry had mown the lawn, and prepared an area just right for some chairs and a table, overlooking the renovated fish pond, under the old apple trees with their swelling crop.

They sat their together in the afternoon sunshine, watching the bees coming and going in and out of their new hive. Charlie was fascinated.

'You know, I think I am the happiest I have ever been in my life,' said Harry quietly.

Annie looked across at him with love in her eyes. Belinda moved gently inside her, and she put her hand on her in a protective gesture.

'I agree with you Harry,' she said with a happy smile, 'Everything seems to be working out right for us now, doesn't it? I'm so grateful for our life here in the country. It couldn't be better.'

All that they had gone through together in those dark years of war seemed to be a far off memory, like a bad dream which could now be forgotten. Eric was now at peace, Harry was fulfilled and their family was nearly complete.

Charlie looked up and said,

'You know that Father Christmas can do his magic all through the year don't you? He has with us, hasn't he?'

They nodded in agreement, and gathering up their tea things went inside their cosy home, leaving the hens scratching for grubs and the bees doing their eternal dance.

The early evening light fell across their garden, now full of healthy fruit and vegetables for the family. The cows in the field down the road mooed as they waited for Harry to milk them. A deep peace was all around the sleepy Devon valley.

Harry stepped out of the back door ready for work, and smiled to himself as he went towards the milking shed. A bee flew over and settled down on his sleeve. He looked at it without fear.

Eric was close and smiled with him.

******

15404983R00092

Printed in Great Britain
by Amazon